JMJ

Wingswept

The Dragon and the Dove

~

Thérèse Judeana

En Route Books and Media, LLC

Saint Louis, MO

Make the time

En Route Books and Media, LLC
5705 Rhodes Avenue
St. Louis, MO 63109

Contact us at
contactus@enroutebooksandmedia.com

Cover Credit: Grace Bourget and Thérèse Judeana

Copyright 2025 Thérèse Judeana

ISBN-13: 979-8-88870-232-1
Library of Congress Control Number:
2024945766

Dedication

In reparation to the Holy Face
of Our Lord Jesus Christ,
To dry the tears of Our Lady of La Salette;
To St. Dwynwen, St. Dymphna, and St. Jude;
To the broken hearts that long to fly

"My heart is troubled within me: and the fear of death is fallen upon me. Fear and trembling are come upon me: and darkness hath covered me. And I said: Who will give me wings like a dove, and I will fly and be at rest?" - *Psalm 54:5-7*

"Destroy . . . him that holdeth the sickle in the time of harvest: for fear of the sword of the dove every man shall return to his people, and every one shall flee to his own land." - *Jeremiah 50:16*

Cast of Characters

Alandis Adrastėja – A young daughter of Erevale, at 19 she finds herself dramatically changing her future.

Ean Adrastėja – Alandis' only sibling, her older brother.

Adrastėja – Alandis' father.

Lord Arvan – the Lord of the Ahren people of Isola, who keeps a home for travelers and those who are wounded or weary of life.

Doctor Guéreur – The man who performed the life-saving operation to save Alandis in her childhood, utilizing the dragon-blood amber.

Trys Saules – Alandis' first love, one of the angelic Ahren people.

Enara Saules – Trys' sister, Alandis' closest friend in Erevale.

Zain Solavier – One of Lharmeval's guardian warriors, he's commanded to remain at Alandis' side in her efforts against the dragons.

Dlam U'Dell – one of the infamous Black Knights of Marèn, who seems to bear a hatred of dragons.

Table of Contents

I

Borne on the Wind

They'd told her if she lost it, she'd be broken forever. The warning ran on, humming in the background of Alandis' mind, echoing until she no longer took notice of it.

"It" was the implant. It had barely saved Alandis' life when she was only five, and her heart had nearly died. It had been a miracle at the time, the utilization of dragon-blood, the amber resin from the bones of dragons.

They had said that it captured the energy of the sun, which used to heal the dragons and give them strength, lasting even through the night. For Alandis, it kept her heart beating.

They had also warned her that as an experiment the resin may flow into her veins and form a symbiotic relationship with her heart. Alandis figured that didn't really matter; she was alive, and she never felt anything change. The only item of note had been the streaks of amber-fire which had appeared in her hair, but that could have been genetics.

The maiden lightly touched the glossy gemlike resin at the pit of her throat. It faintly glimmered and winked, like the reverberation of the ancient dragon-call – dragons had either been extinct for a long time or had flown north to the regions of ice.

The implant's weight still felt alien, and there were times when, unfocused, she could barely keep from tearing it out. She would have died, so she desisted.

Her fingers trembled with the effort to leave it alone as she dropped her hand, but a timely interruption came in the form of Enara Saulės: of equal age, she was the closest Alandis came to calling sister.

"Alandis? We're all waiting for you," Enara offered, advancing. Her thick, loosely-braided tresses swung over her shoulders, set like woven gold against the high-necked azure gown of the untroubled style common in Lharmeval. Enara was gladdened by the quick smile of welcome. "You know you shouldn't vanish from gatherings like this."

The words were a chilling stab of pain, which made the gem's dim glow flicker despite Alandis' unchanging smile.

"I . . . know. I thought I could get something done."

She gently straightened the beads of the chaplet she was weaving. They were a shapeshifting golden-blue, just like—

"—His eyes. Mm, it's for Trys again, isn't it?" Enara noted, leaning over Alandis' shoulder. The latter instinctively half-covered it and sighed, for Enara already knew. She was Trys' sister, after all.

Alandis smiled at the thought. Like Trys, Enara possessed the grace of the Ahren, the almost-elven; not in life-span, but in grace and gift. They might as well have been angels, so far did they seem to transcend all others, yet they loved so deeply that they forever stooped to the human race, as though there was no distance between them.

She thought of Trys, with his golden hair and radiant eyes, and there always seemed to be light pouring out of him. When he smiled, his eyes might have been the sun. He towered over her, yet as though he was stooping to be with her; he made her feel precious, despite his breezy distance. He listened the way no one else did, and he made her concerns his own.

This had made her fall, and despite all the times others encouraged her not to love him, and the lack of any sign from Trys, every time she tried to let go and prayed to be able to let go, the answer came that her heart was called to his. And so, despite her fears and misgivings, she trusted that she had been made to love him and persisted. She suffered much because of it, learning not to speak of him and to hide her feelings from everyone, even Enara, when she could.

"Mm-hm," Enara murmured, amusing herself by reading the dream written on Alandis' face.

Alandis shook herself and looked to the chaplet in her hand.

"I fear to gift it. He always smiles, yet somehow, I think I discomfort him. He seems to be avoiding me after Masses, and this last time he ignored me. . . I assumed he was only anxious about his trials this week."

"He knows."

Alandis froze.

"He knows you care," Enara said apologetically. "That's why."

The gem sputtered with the skipped beat of panic.

"Don't fear, he's still your friend. He just. . . doesn't know what to do about it."

Alandis' lip nearly bled from the force with which she bit it. For a moment, she'd thought that was a good thing, that he knew – but now she realized that she'd gone from wanting to see him to wanting to hide. Instead, she stowed the beads and arose, counting the seconds well, for Enara had been right about her isolation.

In Lharmeval, if one wandered from a gathering, it might as well have been a cold shoulder. It was one of the foundations of society, meant to foster gentleness, peace, virtue, and companionship, by always doing one's work or play with at least one other. The convents and monasteries were thus disposed; therefore, the realm saw it wise for all.

It was, and yet Alandis seemed an outsider, for she could never make her thoughts known; no one took her seriously, and no one shared her hobbies or dreams, so what was she to do? Every time she mingled with others, she'd burn herself.

Alandis knew she had become a puzzle for others. They called her the Dove, as was her namesake, for she was content and quiet; she loved all, and yet, as the doves after their release, was rarely seen, rarely heard. She kept to herself when she could, fearing the inevitable failures she'd make, the thousands of torments and scars she'd give herself in the following years for a misstep in word or action.

But Trys. . . Trys was the love of her heart. While he never came to find her, he was the only one who never offered her any accidental harm.

Against all these, Alandis saw herself with pain, knowing that each time she strayed away, she was further from belonging. She feared that the love of others was only a veil of pity and confusion, even if she knew it wasn't true.

"Never mind," Enara drew Alandis out of her thoughts. "Give it to him anyway, and he'll love it."

Alandis hesitated for a breath, ready to run away from Trys once more.

Love him as I love you, the whisper came, and with an aching heart, Alandis took up the cross again.

"I will return with you," she said aloud, placing the beads in the embroidered pouch at her waist.

She took up her seica, one of the few weapons or tools all women were accustomed to. It served as scythe and staff, practical for life in the hilly woodlands where foliage might get in the way. The blade was sheathed in a thin coating of lightweight birchwood in tinted colors, intricately carven as the women loved beautiful things, and was bound to three sturdy brooches of decorative design which could be clasped at shoulder and waist to secure the seica when not in use.

"Good girl," Enara smiled, "they'll be wanting to release the doves, so let's hasten."

She led the way out of the studio and under the swaying trees of Erevale.

Erevale was a village south of the slopes of Erenni, mount of the citadel and royal city. Unlike the splendor of her neighbor, Erevale laced the rambling, sporadic woodland like the many streams which ran through it, silver light glowing off every bark and branch. Here, the wind blew in song amid a chorus of chaffinches, blackbirds, goldfinches, and robins, whose songs mixed like a basket of sparkling stones that tumbled down a hillside. The weather was forever mild and cool, and homes and churches lived among the dappling trees as though this were all a great garden.

Paths of lemon-tinted amber wreathed their way through groves of birch and aspen and wild gardens of crocus, lily-of-the-valley, and violets, perched among moss and fern. All paths meandered to the village square, in a glade where the sun fell brightly, leaving rainbows in the fountain's spray, a fitting greeting from the church steps.

Homes were crafted of the timber of birch and the traditional rosey-violet wood of the *aschura*, unique to Lharmeval. There was a difference in the houses today; streamers of multi-colored, woven ribbons and lace garlanded every door, braided with rue and anemone.

It was the Day of the Doves, and, as Enara had said, the village was impatient to release the doves which had been raised in simulated habitats. These birds were precious in memory to the kingdom, for the first sighting of the land had been the cloud of doves in the trees, with plumage of white, rosy lavender, and ghostly blue. It was the song of these birds that had drawn the shipwrecked colonizers out of a storm to the mount of Erenni, which became the natural fortress and glorious capital, unparalleled in beauty and creative wealth.

The tale had been immortalized in the kingdom's standard, upon which a dove winged low over mounting waves, on a breeze bound with loosened blossoms. They were celebrated, too, in festivals such as this day's: once a merely dove-themed celebration of God's mercy and blessing, over the past few centuries predators to the doves' young had arisen, leading to their breeding in simulated habitats. Today, the past season's young would be released into the wild.

Even now, Alandis and Enara could hear the familiar canticle ringing faintly through the trees.

In misty morning
Before all awake
I rise to sing a song of hope
Heart so chained, missing the key,
Arise and sing, mourning with me,
The day All-Love died on history's tree.

~

This love I sing
It bore all pain
So that all might be healed again
Drawn out of fury, out of flood,
No bark, nor thorn, nor shedding rose-bud
Will hide from us the price of His Blood.

It was part of the song of the mourning dove, one of comfort, hope, and memory; a song which all knew by heart, but a gust of wind carried the words back whence they'd come as Enara hummed. The snowflake-blooms of the lily bounced and swayed in the breeze, sending its sweet perfume like an echo of the bells which were ringing.

Alandis shook her hair out of her eyes and fitted the traditional headband, with its winging earplates and swinging beads, to her brow. It held her hair out of her face while letting it blow freely behind her. Enara never needed one. Her gilded mane seemed to barely billow in the building breeze.

"This wind is a traitor," Enara said aloud, watching as it ripped blossoms from the tallest flowers. "For three days, it's been taking flowers from us."

"I still love it," Alandis answered softly, watching the flowers billow as colored snow. "Just as long as it does no harm."

"You are a dear," Enara murmured affectionately.

"Enara!"

A welcome voice floated to them from behind, and footsteps among the dripping grass warned them of a follower.

"Trys Saulės, are you really this late?" Enara asked without turning her head.

"Verily," and Trys dropped a kiss on his sister's hair before half-hesitantly turning his gaze to the other maiden.

Alandis' deepening twilight eyes showed her trepidation before Trys could have missed it. His quick smile erased Alandis' fears.

"It seems I'm in good company," he noted with a teasing bow.

"Blame Alandis, she isolates far too much. Now, it's not like you to be late, brother."

Trys shot the aforementioned a scolding look before answering, "It's this wind—"

He stooped over them shieldingly as another gust shocked the trees, rattling the branches and sending squirrels scurrying for shelter.

"I had word that it's hastening erosion on the island coasts. I need to get someone out there to help reinforce the villages before they crumble off the face of Lharmeval."

Alandis ducked her head as the wind lashed the beads of her headband against her face. Even Enara was catching up her hair in both hands to keep it from blowing in her eyes.

"It seems like a storm!" Enara called.

"We haven't had a bad one since before I was born," Alandis protested.

The wind died as abruptly as it had begun, leaving her raised voice ringing among the chilled trees.

Indeed, Lharmeval enjoyed such mild weather that storms were merely rain, and never in force. The wind, however, was ominously promising a change.

"I haven't seen any storm clouds building, but I'm sure something is coming," Trys said grimly, but his mood lifted as swiftly as the wind as they entered the glade where the village had gathered.

Lights had been strung among the blossoming trees bordering the river, and among the gaily colored tents with pennants and booths of hidden treasures and Lharmeval's favored delicacies, children ran, dragging feather doves through the air on beaded strings. Silver cages filled with singing, waiting doves were held in the center of the glade, awaiting the moment of freedom; but the wind was ripping at the waving ribbons, dragging men and women this way and that, and threatening to cast over any of the tents at random will. Yet through this came the silver sound of lute, lyre, and flute, somehow at home among the wind.

Enara departed to rejoin the volunteers, with a look and a nod for Alandis: a reminder of the chaplet half-forgotten.

Trys stopped to assist in righting an overturned table. Alandis scooped up the fallen armful of red roses, replacing them in their amber vase, thankfully unbroken.

Plucking the broken petals, the girl waited nervously, never certain if Enara was right. What if he truly did ache every time she hung around him?

But he had turned and was facing her before she could realize, and she hastily held out the chaplet to him, flustered.

"I only just finished it, so it isn't blessed."

"Aw, thank you, Alandis. I can always have it blessed."

The wind was picking up once more, and as Trys held out his hand, a whistle came, the silver peal of a bell, and the air was filled with a thousand fluttering feathers of cream and mist and rose.

The pair's eyes were drawn upwards as the young doves struggled against the winding gale, catching in the trees and laced boughs. They shivered there, waiting for the next moment of stillness, confused, and leaving Alandis aching for them.

"Poor Mielė! You always were such a dove," Trys read her gaze. "They'll be well once the wind is down."

He took the beads from her hand and held them before his laughing eyes, noting the coloring.

"Did you gather these stones yourself?"

Such stones could only be found in the alpine streams and on the shore, and Alandis had spent many hours in searching.

"I had been hunting since last spring. The jeweler was kind enough to tumble them for me."

Trys smiled at the work she had done, but with a shiver of something else that made her ask shyly whether he liked it at all.

"How would you think it necessary to ask? It was sweet of you. As I said, you have always been the Dove, Mielė," Trys said quietly with a half smile, though he was turning away, distractedly looking to the others who milled under the blossoming trees.

"Don't let me detain you," Alandis said, with all the sweetness of before, but only the gem reminded that she feared how he felt.

No one ever seemed to notice how the gem repeated what was inside, and for that Alandis was grateful. Maybe no one made the connection, and thought it dappled with the sunlight blowing through the trees.

He glanced at her, almost sharply as though he suspected, but pocketed the chaplet as they were interrupted by Änjorën, one of Trys' favored companions in recreation.

"The doves are unusually spooked," Änjorën murmured, greetings aside.

"It's merely the wind. They wouldn't have it so often in their habitats," Trys replied.

"I think not – they were uneasy even in habitat, and I hear there were repeated attempts to escape. Some injured themselves on the glass walls."

"I said they shouldn't have used glass walls," Trys shook his head. "Perhaps they sense the storm."

"If there *is* one," Änjorën said darkly. He scanned the clear sky. "After three days of this, we should be seeing something by now. I hear tell of isolated thunderstorms in the northeast, in the very least, of a violence unmatched in our history. *Thunderstorms.* The smoke in the air – can you smell it? It's being brought on the wind from the provinces of Lieuvieta and Tryshek. I've never known even our occasional thunderstorms to light fires. It's enough that some are asking Father Arman to hold a vigil tonight. Mark my words, Trys, someone has to batten down each province before whatever it is comes down to us."

"Pray tell, I'm not elected."

Trys was looking at the river. It pounded and twisted in a way unaccustomed, as disturbed as the birds in the trees. Parents were forever pulling children away from the banks, and someone at last had the thought to bar the children within the gathering by the collapsible fences used to safely graze sheep and cattle within the woods.

The doves, finally finding a breath of still air, arose with a cry and departed south, leaving the woodland empty of their mournful calls.

"South? Since when do they not stay?"

It was said under his breath, and neither Änjorën nor the silent Alandis offered an answer.

"Well, that's that," Änjorën declared, once the surprise of the flock's departure had subsided. "I'd best return to the fields, and since you're so late, Trys, I won't ask for your company."

He wandered off, leaving Trys gazing at the shuddering clouds overhead.

A touch on his arm reminded him that Alandis was there. He looked round with a laugh.

"Still here, are you?"

Alandis drew back in apology, realizing he must not have meant, nor wanted her to stay.

"Forgive me, I wasn't sure if I'd taken my leave, and – it's only I hardly see you ever since you started in the shoring guild – I miss you."

She halted, having little idea where or how that had been said.

Trys shook his head sharply, looking to the rest of the gathering.

"I know you do, Alandis. I have to go."

A feeling of ice seemed to strike the air and froze Alandis where she stood as Trys left her without another word.

It was the first time he'd ever left her in pain.

"I did. . . hurt you," she whispered dazedly, and only the wind heard her.

II

Just a Hint of Flame

Alandis found herself in her gazebo that evening, long after the sun had fallen, leading the stars out to dance. Her room was separated from the main house, for homes were a complex like a blossoming vine; a rustic path wound up a low mossy ridge, where her room and open-air veranda lay beneath a woven canopy of birch and aschura, framing the stars and leaves overhead.

A stream spilled below the terrace, its silvering-sound usually soothing to her ear, but tonight it only led her mind to deeper thoughts. She plucked one of the rosy morning-glories from its twining vine and let it fall to the water below. It swiftly vanished out of sight.

How long she had wandered through wind and wood she did not know. The thought that she'd disturbed the earthly light of her heart, had so distressed him that he'd had to bear her presence with learned patience—it might have seemed a little thing to anyone but the Dove. Her heart had broken repeatedly in the walk she'd taken, abandoning the festivities in isolation once more as she cried to know whether she'd disturbed the heavenly light of her heart, too, in failing to understand if the words she heard were only imagination.

Her heart had superficially healed every time her tired mind had found something else to notice; then it had reopened, until her heart was exhausted and she'd wondered whether the dragon-blood had ceased its aid.

Trys – her beloved Trys – her heart cried, and all at once it twisted in violence. She longed to forget him, the one person whom she'd never thought she'd fail. She longed to fly with the fleeing doves, finding some life in which she could cease to be the sweet but useless Mielė, who had chosen to live quietly with no accomplishment, lest she leave her family and Trys.

Her thoughts were churning like the bubbling stream below her. She didn't blame Trys for her pain the way another would have. It was all her own, to have tried so hard. If it was true that the voice she'd heard had been her imagination and not God, many more things were built on sand. She clutched at the balustrade as the ground seemed to crumble beneath her.

"Father, Mother, Scier!" she closed her eyes and begged for someone to halt the shifting sand. The wind whispered in reply and tousled her hair in a kiss.

A luna moth landed beside her and crept to her hand with questioning antennae; Alandis stroked its drooping luminescent wings as her tears faded.

Yes, if she left, she would grow, leave Trys free, and test the merit of her feelings. Of the seven provinces, one would harbor her well, she mused. She would travel east from Clariègia, through the provinces of Min-doul and Nvilna, until she reached the coast of Nèraamin. It was the farthest she could travel without heading to the stormy north, and there was the cloistered, quiet school of arts she'd used to think of attending.

She would go there now, and busy herself, and, she hoped, become a better version of herself. One which, she prayed, would no longer be of pain to others. She watched the luna moth flit away and wondered whether she could mirror its transformation.

To leave at once was the point of difficulty. There was only one way to secure it, and she prayed it would not be rough on her family. Children of

Erevale were accustomed to claiming a grace of discovery in their eighteenth year, a self-challenge to free themselves by what they'd find most difficult, to discover who they were. This was a grace which Alandis had been content not to claim, and so her eighteenth year had passed in her sweet, quiet pleasures at home. If she claimed this grace now, she knew that while it might not come easily, it would not be fully contested.

She bent her head and the breath of prayer that escaped her lips floated on the softly singing wind, asking for blessing and clarity.

It was all she could do, she thought and hoped as she raised her eyes to the stars above. She would test herself and find a better way to live; she would spare Trys from her presence; she would free others of her failures, at least for a little while. Maybe it would help her to not fail again – she might be failing by departing, but that could not be helped, it seemed.

So it was that when she went down to the house at last, casting open the doors, she held her seica flat in both hands as she paused on the divide between homelight and moonlight.

Her brother Ean straightened from tending the fire and at once made a gesture as though to stop her. Mother and Father, too, arose, Mother with a little sigh that was half a sob.

Alandis half-dropped her head, wishing she could apologize, but she had made up her mind. The Dove could not forever be silent.

She planted the seica against the stone tiles with a rap.

"As a child of Erevale, it is time that I be borne on the wind. I claim the grace of discovery! I will go out from Erevale and into the farthest countries, and I will remain there until I have been tested. A week from hence, I shall go to the school of Era'menu, if it pleases you."

For a moment there was only a sigh as her father bowed his head. When he raised it again, he said gravely, "My Dove, I know this is because of Trys. If he knew that he had made you feel so, he would prevent you from leaving."

"Daddy. . . I need to go, let me go. If I am your dove, release me! I will come back, as they always do. Even this dove needs to feel the breeze beneath her."

Her father gazed into her pleading eyes and saw that she did not believe that Trys would hold her back.

"I release you, Mielé."

"Mielé -" Her mother stopped, then came and kissed Alandis' brow. "I am proud of you to be willing to test yourself. Only. . .never run away."

Ean said nothing. He knew, as Alandis did, that no one had expected her to leave; they didn't want her to. Neither did he.

They also knew that she was running, running to outrun her heart and her mind, and running away from Trys.

She didn't tell herself that.

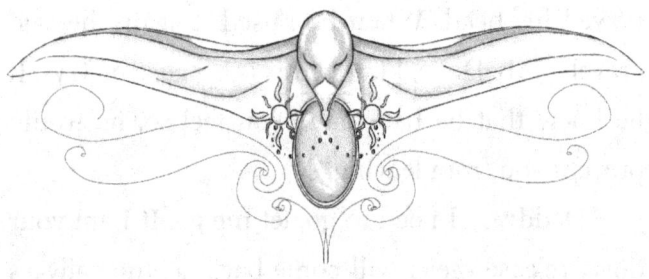

Three days later, the chilled violet veil of dawn found Alandis wrapped up in velvet cloak and hood, riding with Ean towards Erenni, from whence caravans frequently departed for the outer provinces. One was leaving later that morning for Nvilna, hence why her departure had not been put off a full week.

They were already leaving Erevale's woodland. Ean had spoken very little on the ride, silent as the night on which Alandis had claimed her grace. It was clear he neither wanted to challenge his sister's decision nor let her go.

Alandis had informed no one of her leave-taking, even Enara, for fear that Trys would hear of it. She bit her lip, unable to still her mind from wondering what he might say and do; part of her hoped he'd be pained so that she'd know he cared, but he would have blamed himself, and that was the last thing she wanted. She prayed that he would understand she was alright with leaving.

She hoped she was.

She had packed lightly, with only the clothing and personal items she could bear easily in a knapsack. The school would provide her with all she needed for her studies, so she would need none of her own supplies. She'd dressed in rose-dyed doe-skin, embroidered in traditional style, with beaded purse at her waist, seica clasped to her back, and her crucifix on a beaded rope at her side, for the dragon-blood hindered its wearing over her heart. Winging gauntlets braced her arms, and the headband held back her hair. Practicality and beauty were, to her, of one mind.

The pair had come to the slopes now, and were joining the white cobblestone road, up which a handful of merchants and travelers were already trekking. Perched above on the crest of the hill, the city was rising out of the fog and violet. The first sunrays were gilding it like a clarion-call, a proud, beautiful face behind which royalty of earth submitted to that of Heaven.

Grasping Alandis' shoulder firmly, Ean drew her through the tangle of the early morning bazaar, full of tapestries in the jewel-tones of stained glass, woven crosses and baskets, the latter brimming with breads, fruits, and flowers. Breaking through the sea of good-natured chaos, Ean and Alandis came to the ancient cathedral. It marked the crown of the city square with its braided pillars and lace-work windows, and a trickle of early risers were mounting the stairs to hear Mass.

Brother and sister joined them, glad for a way to fill the silence between them, and Alandis could only guess that Ean was entrusting her to his King as he gazed intently upon the altar.

For her own prayer, Alandis could form no words for all that she might need to say. She found herself trying not to realize the violence with which she was leaving. There was a sense of guilt weighing over her which she could neither shake nor wash away. She must go, she reminded herself.

Drawn out of fury, out of the flood,
No bark, no thorn, nor shedding rose-bud
Will hide from us the price of His Blood.

The song seemed the only words she could phrase – Yes, even here in her pain she had to see the price of His Blood. She would follow through with her difficult decision, if only to be tested, for somehow despite her failures and lack of tact with Trys, she had been worth the Ultimate Price.

She joined Ean's intent stare, so much so that he needed to gently shake her, for she had not noticed that Mass was over; sunlight was streaming through the windows now, and she could hear the sparrows chirping just outside.

"You need to eat," Ean said shortly, once they were outside the doors. He let out his breath. "Mielė, tell me you're going to take better care of yourself than you have the past few days, or I'll truly hate that you're going."

"I promise."

"At least that," he muttered, and handed her the fried grape flatbread he'd bought. There was fresh water from the fountain, and they let their mounts drink from the adjacent trough.

When Alandis glanced up, Ean had vanished, and the growing bustle of the bazaar aided little in finding him with her eyes. Her brother was not gone long, however, and when he returned, he held something in his hand, but only took his stallion's reins and Alandis' hand, and guided them out of the square into one of the lower terraces of the city.

The caravan of brightly-painted wagons was almost ready to go; most members were families returning home or on their way to visit relatives. Three knights were mounted, idly watching the final preparations. These were the traditional guards in case of the occasional highwaymen, and the only

reason Ean was even slightly willing to leave her
there. He stood a moment, clasping her hand.

"Mielė -" Ean put something in her hand. It was
a strand of lapis and amber beads. Alandis had
possessed such a necklace a long time ago, when she
had been given the implant, but had subsequently
lost it to one of the forest streams.

"Ean – I love you."

He nodded but wouldn't meet her gaze, leaving
her to suspect there were tears there.

"If you ever want to come home," he said gruffly,
"send a dove and I'll come and get you."

Alandis' head drooped, for she felt the words
neither could say about staying, or of running away.
She had committed. She raised her head and Ean
was able to meet her gaze.

"God keep you while I'm away," Alandis whispered.

"May Scier and Mother watch over you."

Alandis embraced him. The caravan was
moving out; she mounted and joined. Glancing over
her shoulder, she saw Ean standing high on the
terrace stairs to watch. He lifted his hand in farewell.
It was the last Alandis would see of him for many
months.

The ride passed quietly for several days. The wind was calmer, though there was a dark line on the northern horizon, and smoke still lingered on the air.

Alandis befriended several of the mothers and children, leading her to pass her time assisting with meals and keeping rambunctious little ones occupied. Her peace, however, seemed to fade rapidly with each step she took. Her heart ached for the man she loved, for the seeming act of "betrayal" she'd played him, for the sorrow she'd felt in Ean and her parents. Nightmares riddled her sleep, and the day held a clinging sense that something was wrong.

Every few minutes her heart lightened at the thought of turning back. She could apologize to Trys instead of running away – and then she remembered that she couldn't turn back, not on her own, and she needed the change. So, she pressed onwards.

The fifth day fell differently. It had begun much the same with an early start, a sprinkle of rain, and the making of good time. As dusk fell, however, the wind whipped through the tall grasses. Setting up camp had to be delayed and shelter sought in the forest.

There was a sound encased in the hissing breeze, something Alandis could not identify and yet she was sure it was there. Nervously, she called the wandering children back into the lamplight and aided in bundling them up into the wagons.

A shout carried back to them from the head of the line. All halted.

"What is it?" one of the knights called, riding ahead.

Alandis pressed closer through the wagons to hear.

". . . I don't know, I saw something moving and could have sworn I saw fire." This was from one of the other knights, the youngest of the three.

"If you're seeing will-o-the-wisps again – this isn't even a bog, Marté. Or at least there wasn't one."

"Will-o-the-wisps nothing! They don't bear the shadow of a beast about them, Arvel," Marté said quietly.

"Luka!" Arvel called back. "Bring a lantern and let's see. Fellows, keep the ladies and youngsters close in the wagons, just in case."

Alandis untied her mare, who was shivering as though she sensed what had been seen.

"Ssh, nothing will hurt you, Sissi," Alandis murmured, smoothing the velvet muzzle and looking ahead into the darkness.

"There is a bit of a marsh from the rain," Arvel called finally. "Only a few inches. See anything, Luka?"

"Noth-whoa, *whoa-!*"

Another shout, a screaming blast, and the acrid crackling, ripping open of an explosion sent men scrambling, horses rearing as flame burned out the night and seared the trees, smoke and steam rising in one cloud of tattered hue.

"Get them out of here!" Luka yelled, waving the caravan back as a looming shadow ran through the flame.

The caravan careened out of the forest outskirts as a track of flame nearly spliced it apart. Alandis was not so lucky in escape, for she and Sissi were blocked out by the firewall.

Sissi shrieked and wheeled away as her rider tried to find a way around, running from whatever was behind them. There was a sound of pounding, like a drum amid a thundering volcano, but it soon ceased.

By the time they were free of the fire, the caravan was no longer in sight. Not a sound of it could be heard. Even Sissi's ears swiveled in vain.

Whether the caravan had escaped, Alandis had no way of knowing. She knotted her fingers in Sissi's mane and touched the crucifix at her side.

"May they be as safe. . . or safer, than we are. Please, keep them that way." She was certain that her words were heard.

Alandis no longer knew what was north and what was south, for smoke and cloud dimmed the stars until she could not hope to find her way. All she could do was try to find the road.

They tramped through forest and fen for hours, far into what must have been morning, with no light and only Sissi's eyes to see by. All was still. Even the birds were silent, leaving only an ominous cracking in the trees, as though they whispered of the still-unidentified danger. Leaves crunched underfoot, seemingly far too loud in the empty night.

After some time of clambering down a moss-covered slope, the land leveled out. There was a dim streak of lightness underfoot that told Alandis it was the road at last – *a* road, at least.

"North, south, east, west, I know not," she sighed to Sissi, and sent a glance skywards. "If this be the wrong road, let it be the right one in Your eyes."

She turned Sissi towards the leftwards running lane. The mare snorted hardly a mile later and drew back. Alandis squinted into the sudden fog.

The violent amber of a direction sign seemed to blaze through. Relieved, Alandis drew at the reins. At last, she would know what direction they might have taken.

Then the lights blinked.

A shadow stretched overhead.

It was then that Alandis knew.

Dragons had returned to Lharmeval.

III

Waylaid by a Matter of Dragons

Eerie whistling filled the night. Crackling as of shattering metal echoed as the scales raised, revealing bleeding amber and rivulets of blinding starlight.

Two slow measured strides brought the hulking shadow over Alandis as wings raged by living fire unfurled to frame the moon that now appeared between clouds. As the starlight cracked across its face, the head's silhouette was burst by glowing teeth.

Sissi reared. In her freeze of shock, Alandis let the reins slip through her fingers and didn't have time to find her seat before her shoulders collided with the ground. The air went out of her lungs sharply by the force of her fall, as though filled by the emptiness of the sky.

As Sissi leaped away, Alandis instinctively threw her hand over the amber to shield it, even then probing its surface for damage, but despite the pain that had gone through her, there was no harm done.

She grasped her crucifix with her other hand. She found herself numb, stuck on the first five words of the Ave, unaware of anything but the dragon's massiveness.

Alandis knew from legend that dragons had only one weakness: a loosened scale. Her heart sank as she noted the deliberate cracking between the plates, a clear sign that the dragon had no such weakness between its scales.

The drake's breath rattled as it unmasked itself from the fog, head leaning in until its heat was scorching her face.

Its form was simultaneously lionesque in power, lupine in grace, three times taller than she, and she couldn't make out where the tail ended.

It was a drake, though Alandis had no way of knowing its wings were only half-formed, its body only that of three years—three years and seven months to be exact, but Alandis didn't exactly care.

She did a moment later, when it struck her that that knowledge did, in fact, exist in her mind. How she knew that was something she didn't know.

For a moment confusion paused fear, and she forgot the thing walking towards her was probably one inhalation away from killing her. Then the thought of her family, of Trys, finding out that she'd been crushed or singed to death, broke through and hurt her. It hurt her so much that just for a sliver of a breath she admitted to herself that she had run away.

It then struck her that the dragon was indignant at her distraction. She looked up.

"Just give me a moment, won't you?" she exclaimed. Then she remembered it was a dragon, and one doesn't exactly order a dragon to give a moment, not to good effect.

For one hiss it held its breath, eyeing her with what emotion she couldn't tell, and in the mounting silence even Sissi didn't dare to move, and as the trees ceased to creak, terrified of the fire that might end them, the amber eyes slit shut.

It gave a very sharp snort that whipped itself back off the trees, making the leaves rustle far more loudly than they intended. Alandis' body jerked at the deafening sound and heat. Her hand snapped away from the implant. For the first time, its angry red flash keeping tempo with her racing heart, burnt both into her vision and the drake's.

It recoiled with a squawk like a frightened bird, wings half-shielding itself as it shrieked in confusion. It pattered backwards a few paces as Alandis took the chance to drag herself backwards towards Sissi, still poised nervously at the edge of the trees.

With all three of them jumping, Alandis didn't know which was worse: trying to talk to the dragon, or trying to escape on Sissi.

The dragon snaked its neck at her with a snap of its jaws.

"Take it easy!" Alandis exclaimed, jumping again and wondering if her heart would ever stop hurting.

She could have read the question marks all over the dragon's face as it froze in utmost perplexity.

They held a staring contest.

The amber. It had been in the bones of a dragon.

At once Alandis understood that this drake was confused by the melding of human and dragon in one.

"Don't be scared! I'm not going to hurt you, not that I could," she added, wondering whether that was going to help.

Yet, it seemed to, for the dragon rolled its wings uncertainly and at last placed all four paws on the road.

"Um. . . thank you, I think?"

Alandis gingerly edged to stand while the dragon cocked its head. Then it was held right up to her, so close she could barely breathe, examining the flashing implant with a questioning sound.

Alandis could not help but admit that the mass of fiery scales and power had descended into the zone of cuteness, as though that were somehow even remotely possible.

It ended its inspection with a shift from perplexity to utter delight as it spun, puppy-like, as puppy-like as a ten-ton dragon could, interrupted by a growl that reminded her it was, indeed, a dragon, and she was probably imagining things, and she heard, *Tiny human dragon!*

Oh no.

And then it called for Mother.

"No, no, don't call your mother!" Alandis begged in desperation. Despite the drake's sad eyes, it was too late.

Mother was already leaving her perch, as evidenced by the brightly glooming flame approaching through the clouds, and a roar. The latter would have been described as a hurricane of thunder, had Alandis been familiar enough with either. The wind from the dragon's wings cast a wave through the trees, threatening to break branch and root in one.

Alandis backed up, but any thought of reaching Sissi was made hopeless, for Mother was three times the size of her son.

"Why me?" Alandis whispered helplessly as she shut her eyes.

Mother's breath came as the rumble of a purr as she listened to her son's excited grumbles, and as the drake hopped onto his mother's shoulders, before Alandis could take a second step back, the talons of a paw as large as her home in Erevale closed about her as she cried out.

Still, she found herself neither crushed nor burnt, only – disconcertingly so – leaving the ground.

All the light, even of the dragon scales, had been closed out. All that remained was the flickering fire of the amber as the air grew colder.

Even the whistling of scales and wings had been dulled inside the cocoon of the dragon's paw, leaving Alandis to find her exhaustion, and the question of whether the dragons were violent or gentle, just for a moment.

Alandis rested her head back against the bracing claws and dreamed of home, wondering if this was why she had left, or was this a scolding for leaving? Trys' eyes seemed to pierce the darkness before her own, replacing the late view of amber terror, and her heart ached . . . then found rest in his gaze and wondered whether he would, indeed, have come. Would he have drawn her out of the growing darkness in her own mind?

She must have slept, just for a moment, for her eyes snapped open against a rush of steam as she was deposited on something soft. The amber had eased its panicked glow and all was dark, save for the rippling of armor on Mother's back.

It was a mountain cave they were in, recently hewn by spiked tail and talons. Alandis had been dropped into the hollow of a shattered stalagmite, cushioned by the rich moss which grew all over floor and ceiling.

Mother stretched out, filling the circumference of the walls with her length. She snorted at the drake, scoldingly, yet Alandis knew there was praise, too, for his first solo adventures. She watched a moment, for both were terrifying to behold, but with each other, they were only mother and son.

She missed her mother. She sighed, for she was too tired to fight her presence among the dragons. Every ounce of mind had been worn out of her and her lids soon closed against the dim glow of Mother, and the rumbling that filled the room.

IV

Twist of Fate

Morning found Alandis dragon-free and reunited with Sissi, as she reached the first semblance of civilization. In the glacial valley, dairy farms were scattered among swathes of wildflowers, but Alandis' eyes were too tired to read the directional. Sissi, too, was plodding at her slowest pace, only drawn further by the visual promise of the green grass ahead.

Alandis had woken early that morning in the cave, and summoning all her courage, had managed to carry on a conversation with the dragons. It was difficult to get Mother to stop blocking the cave exit, for it seemed both believed her to be some sort of infant dragon – a very strange sort – in need of adoption. This was flattering in one sense and Alandis had been equally confused by their affection. All she had ever heard of dragons was their vicious and destructive nature, but of course among themselves they would be as loving as any other creature.

The conversation had been, on Alandis' part, an attempt not to sound as intimidated as she felt looking upon dragon and drake. At the same time, she now harbored a strange fondness for both.

Studying the implant, the drake had asked Mother whether humans, too, had dragon-amber in their veins. Mother had swung her head down to look into Alandis' eyes, as closely as she could manage.

How do you bear dragon-blood in your veins?

Alandis had steeled herself. Would they kill her in fury, that it had come from the bones of a dragon?

"It isn't of me," she had answered slowly. "I understand if you'll be angry. It was given to me as a child to keep my heart alive when it was damaged."

Mother had become very still. Her eyes had flashed and without a sound, she had unblocked the cave entrance. The drake had backed up against his mother's side.

In that moment Alandis felt their fear of humans, and yet they were so much larger, so much more destructive and powerful that it seemed almost laughable compared to the fear they had placed on this corner of Lharmeval.

Silently, Alandis had left. Sissi, never well on her own, must have attempted to follow the dragon's path, for she was discovered near the foot of the mountain when Alandis had descended.

Now, as Alandis looked upon the valley, she saw signs of flame and wind: scorched fields and barns, splintered fences, uprooted trees that crushed both stables and stone walls, and broken petals lying all across the ground, torn from the anemones, lilacs, and blooming cherries. Boulders had tumbled from the mountains, crushing habitations, and everywhere she looked, the dirt had churned into mud. Even the grass had been beaten down.

A ranger was kicking aside the crumbled bricks of the wall and forcing the fallen planks to render some service in penning-in the straying animals. He was one of the Zaindaria, custodians of the realm and general assistants of the people in times of trial.

"Where am I?" Alandis asked him wearily. "I can't read the directionals."

He dropped the last beam and regarded her with dry amusement.

"Of all the places you want to be, lass, this isn't one. You're on the coast of Lieuvieta near Isola. The dragons have come."

He said it ominously, as though he expected she didn't know; she wouldn't have, if not for the drake. Was he trying to frighten her? He had a warm smile though, and was unlikely to be any older than Ean or herself, so she guessed no.

"Yes, I noticed." She eyed the uprooted trees. "Tell me, where can I go? I can't turn back in this state."

He looked at her, calculatingly.

"There's an Ahrenian citadel, or retreat, if you prefer, in the crest of Isola. It's suffered no damage as yet, but Isola has seen the most of the dragons. It's the farthest east you can go from any given point in Lharmeval, if that appeals to you, and the Ahren ever house those who seek shelter. My duties call me there, so I may guide you, if you wish."

The farthest from home, the farthest from Trys, her mind repeated like a bell that wouldn't be silenced.

Farthest? The challenge to her heart drew her over the channel.

So it was that Solavier had guided her up the far hills and they looked upon Isola. The far-eastern province was separated from the realm by a wide channel, save for a narrow, part-times flooded, land bridge.

"I would not tarry in this land," Solavier warned. "It's far too dangerous here, and those who have been able to leave already have. The rest keep on surviving, living in terror, and to step outside seems to them to chance fate. My Zaindarian brothers and I have been hard-pressed to aid them. There is not much to be done against these dragons."

He crossed the channel with her. On the other side, all semblance of the country she knew vanished. The language on the directionals became solely that of Ahrenian; the Lharmevalan architecture was replaced by the ancient style, soaring yet vanishing back into the moss and greenery into which they were settled.

The damage, too, was unlike that she'd seen in Lieuvieta. Relief efforts were to be seen in every corner, drawing villagers and animals from rubble, and shoring up damaged houses.

Shoring made her think of Trys, and just for a moment she superficially hoped he wouldn't be called to this northern territory. She knew that it wouldn't happen. His guild was only in the west, never to the south, north, or east. She was safe.

Her heart still plummeted.

"I'll come back once I've left you at the House," her companion said quietly, looking with pity on a gathering of weeping children. "There's much to be done here, and the dragons must be stopped somehow. They are far larger than legend, and deadlier. Never could a man kill it by sword or arrow, without being wiped off the face of Lharmeval first. The very elements and roots have been twisted to obey them – fire, storm, wind, tree, and water. Even the shadows are darker now. The livestock and the fish and the sea are being hunted to extinction, and we'll be blessed if they don't come for us all after. Every day, every child wakes and wonders if it will be the last morning, if their cat will be dead by night, their homes still standing, and when night falls, they wonder if they'll ever awaken and whether they'll feel the pain. Would that I could kill each dragon to end that!"

Solavier sighed, weight leaning heavier in his saddle, but he said no more on the matter.

Alandis dropped her head and wondered, too, what anyone could do. . .what could she do? The amber seemed to weigh heavier and heavier upon her heart, crushing the pain of Trys. It was not something to be thought of here, even if she did find the memory of his face in the blue sky.

The House, in truth a community, was nestled among the crests of the low mountains, with the view of the ocean on one hand, the valley on the other, and sweeping mountains to either side. It was a natural citadel, for even a dragon couldn't have found its way between the peaks.

It was quiet, the kind of quiet that's rarely found, save in a church emptied between Masses. Even nature seemed to sing in a lower voice, soothing rather than wild. Alabaster villas and alpine gardens mounted the slopes amid a rampant tumbling of currants, elders, and roses, braced by gilded rowans and proud pines. The great courtyard was ringed by a walking colonnade, rimmed by pools streaming from the fountain.

All was still, save for the methodical strolling of couples and the Ahren elders, garbed in springtime hues. Trys and Enara had never worn Ahren attire. They'd assimilated into the Erevale culture out of love and a desire not to seem otherworldly, as they truly were. Alandis could see now what that unhumbled glory would have been like.

In every face she saw the echo of theirs, but with something like moonlight and starlight, held in the depths of a still pool, in their eyes. Robes with draping sleeves were that of the ancient royals, banded about the waist, not with the Lharmevalan-embroidered sash, but a wide silken band, tapestried in natural motifs and bound with a braided cord of rose-gold and silver. Their winged sandals, too, were of metallic leather. It was an ethereal blend of affinity with nature in simplicity, and something of the regal sunrise.

Each turned to gaze at her, filled with the same fascination and affection that Trys and Enara had always given. They turned back from meeting her, however, when chimes rang softly down from the highest home. The slender spires, here called spinnerets for their silken, woven look, spoke of a church within.

Solavier pulled at her reins, drawing her out of distraction.

"This way," he said gently. "The homelander's house is here, where you'll find rest. Tomorrow, you'll either find yourself on the road or bound here by the dragons. Best if you rest at once."

He left her on the porch as someone came and, with a soft word, led Sissi away. The warm lights inside were inviting as one of the young attendants drew her in. A room was found, white as a breath of pure air, and Alandis took her second, much needed rest.

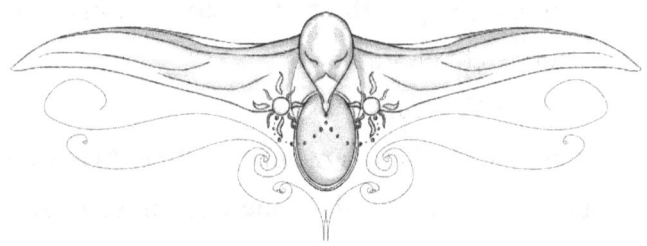

I ought to send a dove, Alandis thought, standing on the wrap-around parapet of the home. The wind was again murmuring, and the golden sky marked the turning to evening. Her family would have expected word from the school by now. She drew the little enameled pen and scroll from her pocket and would have put ink to paper if a startled sigh hadn't stopped her.

It was a man, not one of the Ahren, but one of the many doctors and learned who took meditational retreats here in the mountains. His garb was that of a northerner, but the blue band on his arm told her he was a doctor.

He was not just any doctor, either. Even after fourteen years, the face with its spectacles and now-deeply-grayed beard was unforgettable. His was the face that had bent over her with comforting promises as she'd fallen under the herbal anesthesia.

Alandis dropped the pen in surprise, and the man stooped to pick it up.

"Doctor Guéreur?"

"The amber. You can only be little Alandis!" There was a smile, but his tone was unnecessarily sober.

"The same," Alandis answered respectfully. "I never thought I'd be seeing you again after you retired. But you still wear the band?"

"I un-retired," he answered with a little smile. "Too many need me, and I've been teaching at the schools in the North, for great is our need for another generation in medicine. I've been on retreat here…with what has been happening lately, my skills are needed."

The way he looked at her was unnerving. There was no time for her to ask why.

A scream of ire rang through the clouding sky.

Alandis whipped around to see the beast shoot low over the mountaintops, grazing trees with its wings and snapping them into splinters. It was Mother.

"God help us," the doctor murmured. "There will be deaths, this time."

Alandis looked at him sharply.

"Maybe not!"

Before she knew what she was doing, she had reached through the window, taken her seica from the table where it rested, and was out of the House running for the road. At least Sissi's fear was no match for her loyalty. A whistle brought the mare out of the stables, having kicked open the stall door and knocked several attendants over in the process.

"*Vala*, Sissi, run as swiftly as you might!"

Visions of the weeping children flit before her eyes. That wasn't going to happen again, not if God would let the amber speak His mind.

V

Dove into Dragandrea

When the twist in her life had come, Alandis
had isolated. The dove she'd sent home did not bear
tale of where she was; they never would. Nor would
the school of Era'menu ever see her. She hid her
location and actions from her family, preventing the
facts from being discoverable by Trys. She grieved,
giving up acquiring knowledge of him as she was
wont to do.

Forged in the fire of the dragons, she'd been
made stronger and straighter, still gentle, but she
was the dragon-fighter, the Dragandrea.

That's what *they* called her. Far back in legend
lay some nameless man who had fought the dragons
and cast them from Lharmeval. They'd been smaller
in those days, easier to kill. So, he'd been named the
Dragjauna, something that sounded like hissing
snakes, and it had been the only time the title
Dragon-Lord, the Dragon-Fighter had been given.

Until Alandis' arrival, that is.

Ever since she'd repelled Mother's attack against
the village, the villagers had lifted her up into that

rank. Her costume most days was one they'd given her, mix of legend and Ahren; only the Erevale sash and amber choker still spoke of her home. Platinum and rose were not practical colors for action, but legend called for it, no matter how many times she and the Ahren women had to repair burns and wash out soot and blood and dirt.

Alandis didn't kill the dragons. She couldn't, for most were larger than a houseful of elephants, but the amber helped her to drive them away.

They didn't always listen, the dragons; they were too big to fight realistically, so she'd come to rely on clever roundabouts. Not always her own, for she also relied on Solavier, but only she could get near the dragons while escaping injury.

Usually, anyway. Some of them were spitfires, literally, and would do so regardless of their mood. A burn to a shoulder meant little if it spared the village or countryside. It had become like clockwork, and fending off each dragon was now routine.

Only now she was finding out why -

"Dragandrea -" It was Solavier. "That is, Alandis."

The Dragandrea turned her head to acknowledge him. Solavier was one of the few who used her name, and Alandis was forever relieved to hear it.

"Alandis, I have word from the border. The drake's fires are under control once more."

It had been seven months since that night Alandis had been separated from the caravan and faced the drake alone. He had grown bolder, but he still listened to her, albeit reluctantly.

If humans couldn't kill them, the dragons had little reason to attack as long as other food sources were supplied. Alandis knew that wildlife was growing scarce, but in the very least, dragons could supply themselves solely from solar energy.

"Thank you," she answered, but her eyes saw the expression in the guardian's. It was one she'd hoped to see in Trys' – she shook her head at the thought and dropped her head, troubled.

Solavier came beside her. She had never spoken of Trys to him, but it was not difficult for him to guess her thoughts, especially when the amber sputtered as it did now. The guardian rested his arms on the balustrade. Wind ruffling his hair, his eyes read hers as though they knew more than he would say.

"Do they know? Your family, I mean, do they know where you are?"

"No. If I told them, they'd come here to pull me from danger, and they very well could get hurt!"

Her eyes anxiously studied the stones. She was protecting the village and the surrounding territories, but there was always a risk. Always.

Her family had asked, when she'd never mentioned arriving at the school. She'd only told them that she was on detour farther north, staying in an Ahren village. Her family had begged; Ean had tearfully threatened, even on paper, to find out why she was hiding. By now, they had given up, and it hurt.

Alandis didn't realize she'd said so out loud.

"Lana....you're giving me more reasons that you should send for them."

Alandis smiled.

"Back home no one calls me Lana."

"What do they call you?"

"Mielė, or Dove, sometimes."

"Mm. Mielė is nice."

"It doesn't suit me now, Sol."

"You haven't changed as much as you think. Only sweetness would keep from destroying the dragons, finding that that's alright. You're strong, maybe, but I've seen you cry. You can't stay alone forever, Mielė. Send for them. It hurts me to see you isolate the way you do most days. I love you, Alandis."

Alandis started, finally meeting his gaze. There was no pretense, no flirtation, only those simple words and the clarity in his face as he said them.

"Solavier –" she dropped her head. The memory of how she'd been rebuffed by Trys made her helpless. She couldn't hurt Solavier, nor could she change her mind. Her heart ached worse.

The wind was the only one who spoke for a moment, *love Trys as I love you*, then Alandis raised her head.

"I – can't, Solavier. I'd never want to hurt you. . . the way I was."

"That's alright." Not a trace of a shadow crossed his face. "I'll never force you, nor will I run away."

She felt the last as an arrow.

"I ran away," she said quietly. "I hurt him by trying to love him."

It was the first time she'd spoken of Trys to anyone; the first time she'd admitted in full that she had run.

"Why couldn't you have spoken to him instead?"

Alandis winced, for she had often silenced herself from thinking so.

"I've wondered that, but I was hurt and needed to escape. And if I hadn't," she asked with a hopeless wave towards the village, "what would have come from the dragons?"

"They would have followed you. Just as your own dragons have."

Yes, she had many dragons.

"Lana, if he cared, he would have come back quickly if you'd given him the chance. If he doesn't care, then he's the blindest and dumbest man on earth, and I don't understand how he could hurt you."

He said it so vehemently that Alandis was torn between defending Trys from such a thought and laughing. She did neither and folded her arms again with a sad smile.

"He was good to me always, until I hurt him."

"Then he *would* come for you."

So *they* had said.

"Dragandrea, Zain Solavier!"

The errand-boy was breathless and admiring as he mounted the terrace steps. One of the village boys whose family had suffered in the attacks, the Ahren had felt compassion and employed him to aid his family's recovery.

"Cole, if you don't cease to run withersoever you go, you'll soon be an athlete," Solavier teased.

The boy grinned but bowed in haste.

"The Lord wishes your presence on the upper terrace, if you please."

"Well enough, but catch your breath before you do the slightest thing else," Alandis warned him, and they left him on the terrace.

She remembered the first time she'd met the Lord; it was when she was dying to rest after trying to rein in Mother, that first day.

It had been a fight, convincing Mother to leave the village alone. Alandis had pointed to the drake, and to the crying children, explained how no one knew how to wound, let alone kill, dragons of such size.

Mother had been furious from the living amber placed within a human. Death had been very close until Alandis had scooped a child out of harm's way, and, believing it almost over, gently sung the dove's song to distract the infant.

This love I sing, it bore all pain, so that all might be healed again!

Mother had stopped. Whether she'd been reminded of her own dragon-song to her son, or been moved by the words, or pitied, or held back by angel-hands, Alandis didn't know. The village had been spared.

The Ahren lord had called her to him, and stood, hands clasped behind him as he spoke to Doctor Guéreur; Solavier and another of the Zaindaria stood in the shadows, listening. All turned. Their eyes had fallen on the implant, as they always did.

"My lord, Doctor Guéreur."

"Ara Adrastëja. You've escaped dragons twice and turned them away from harming our village. This is nothing of which we've heard before. What can you say of their weaknesses?"

Taken aback, Alandis had told the Lord of the protected scales.

"I escaped. . . I believe because of the amber. I believe they were confused. They understand our speech, as well."

"No, they do not," the Lord had halted her. "Attempts have been made before, to no avail."

"My lord, I'm going to echo Alandis," Doctor Guéreur had spoken. "It's the amber. It seems I should have watched you longer, Alandis."

His smile was sad as he noted the amber streaks in her hair.

"Oh. . . that was only two years ago."

"It's fully assimilated, then. Many has been the hour which I've been tempted to regret your implant," the doctor murmured. "Yet it saved your life."

Alandis' stomach had twisted.

"Why do you say this?"

"Alandis....they've come because of you. Living dragon-blood is forever sensed by its kind. By placing it within living cells to garner the power of sunlight, it has been reanimated. Had I not believed, along with all our worlds, that dragons were extinct, I would have halted the experiment. By reanimating it in you, it has sent a call to its kind that Lharmeval may once again bear their weight."

Alandis could say nothing, for her blood seemed to freeze, all that save in her heart.

Solavier had breathed something, half-comforting, half-shocked, as he stepped to her side.

"You can't blame yourself for their presence, nor even can I," Doctor Guéreur sighed.

Alandis closed her eyes. She had run from Trys into the arms of fear.

"It must be removed, then," she surmised, voice somehow steady.

"You know as well as I do that you cannot choose your own death. One cannot choose suicide even to save a thousand lives."

Solavier had placed his hand on her shoulder, gripping tightly, and ever after she had wondered, if not asked outright, whether the spiritual danger was why he'd been assigned to remain with her.

'Tell me how the dragon treated you, Alandis. If they're going to attack you, we need to know."

Alandis had hesitated.

"A fire drake, whose mother this was, met me on the road one night. They took me to their cave, seeming to believe that I am some sort of dragon myself, but they know now the source of the amber. I believe it only made them our enemies, yet they would not touch me once out of thrice."

"Indeed," the doctor had nodded slowly. "There is honor among dragons, and though they may now know you are not naturally so, they will hold to their laws. They never fight one another. They will not touch you, or at least they shall not kill you."

"Couldn't we then gather dragon-blood and have others who may be understood?" This was the other ranger, Darje.

"They're already furious with me for bearing it," Alandis murmured.

"Only the living amber, Zain. Raw amber will be of no aid. It took twelve years to be fully accepted by Alandis' cells, and do we have time to wait?"

Lord Arvan had shaken his head.

"We only have one hope, Adrastēja. Find the dragons."

Of all the roads to be placed upon, this had been the one assigned to her. There was no true choice but to offer it up to the One who had given it. She would find the dragons.

Father, help me!

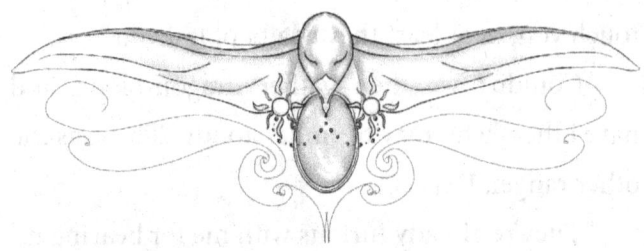

"Ara Adrastėja." The Lord's voice broke Alandis out of her reminiscing.

"Lord Arvan!" she greeted, mounting the last of the stairs, Solavier at her heels. "What do you wish?"

"Not a wish, but news." He guided her eyes to the outside coast. "Many are the words of late which speak of watery ills. Ice in summer, fish scarce as saffron, scales in the waters, evil tides, and waves bordering on tidal."

"A dragon."

"So, it is believed, but it has never been seen, not certainly. At times, sheer wings like frost, or a fin cutting through waves as a shark, but no more. The other wyrms grow accustomed to your voice, if begrudgingly; turn your mind to this marine spectre, if it so be, before those on shore have their lives and livelihoods stamped out."

Alandis' eyes glanced aside to the sea, leaving the Lord's face as he spoke.

There was an eruption in the water below.

Lord Arvan ceased to speak.

"It would seem it has already heard your thoughts, Dragandrea."

"It seems so."

She looked to Solavier, who was testing his blade against the stone.

"It would seem we have our morning interruption."

VI

Wind into Water

The wind rippled Alandis' hair as she and Solavier shot down the hill on horseback. Sol's mount, too, had become relatively used to the dragons, and Sendoa was willing to bear him as close as the dragons would allow.

Alandis' heart beat like a gong in her ears, interrupting every interchanging thought –

I'm going to –

Why does he have to love me?

Have to –

Where is Trys to lift this weight?

Her mind was fogged, a strange cloud of guilt over speaking to Sol at all that morning – to have complained, she thought, and that was always unwelcome – she was supposed to be strong enough for no one to have to know – that's what she thought God wanted, even though she would have said otherwise of anyone else's suffering.

Yes, yes, she had taken all her burdens on her shoulders those seven months, without Trys who had always lifted their weight by a smile and by an "everything will be alright," and she felt crushed by the weight of separation, loneliness, guilt – guilt over the dragons, guilt over running away, guilt over her feelings, guilt over Trys, and now, guilt over Sol.

I know, Alandis, I have to go!

I have to -

I'll never force you, nor will I run away -

I have to -

You were always the Dove, Mielé-

I never –

Blinded, Alandis was only aware they'd reached their destination by Sissi's customary skid-and-rear- abruptly.

She nearly flew over Sissi's head, but Sol's hand must have already been hovering over her arm, because he jerked her back into the saddle.

"Focus!" he commanded, but not unkindly, as though he seemed to know her thoughts. "My Lady, we can't afford to have even the least of us out of action, but you? We may all burn if that happens! Or drown," he added, eyes scanning the scene before them.

Contrary to Alandis' hopes, they were not on the uninhabited southern beaches but across from the lighthouse isle, and pounding waves were frothing and foaming against the wildflower-strewn shores.

The wind was terrific, breaking the stems of the rue, flattening the beach glories, purslane, thrift, and ice blossoms. Once again, the martyred petals flooded the ground like bejeweling blood, cast into Alandis' face and hair. That was not the sight they'd come to see.

Whatever it was, it was thrashing through the water, fins rifting the white waves like maddened sharks, dangerously close to the pier. Too many children had crept out to stare, the boats were tossing and turning, tipping over and straggling their lines and sails, dumping them on the unprepared. The wind rose fiercely, casting rabid foam onto the nearest homes and shops.

"I was calling it to the south," Alandis groaned with sinking heart.

Sol raised an eyebrow.

"Well, these are hardly *tame* dragons, but this is a strange one. Let's go show him – or her – that this is your territory!"

"We have to get it away from the shore! Any clever ideas?"

Sol's eyes went to a fishing barque loaded with that morning's catch, not yet tipped over, for it was anchored up the river that flowed through Isola's heart.

"Yes, one that's fishy."

"Take care of it!" she told him. "I'm going to –"

"Do what you do best, be careful, Lana."

Her breath wavered, and she didn't answer, only dismounted Sissi and ran for the grassy shoreline.

In just a minute, the ship's lines had been cut, and the barque sailed out against the roughening tide, the wind casting the pungent scent of salt and fish far and wide. The waves were swiftly bouncing it away towards the southern beaches. If only the beast who had nearly rid the bay of its marine life would take the bait –

Alandis was sprinting down to the water's edge as it happened. The whirling water ceased, only for a breath, so that for just that space there was an eerie half-silence – then something like a column of sea and sky erupted from the water, crashed over the barque, and in another moment all was still.

The barque had been emptied, only a few of its precious goods still floating on the water. Maybe food was all that the creature had wanted – that, and to see what dragon had dared to challenge it. Surely, it must have known by now whose territory it was.

Alandis' eyes scanned the water and the horizon in vain. Whatever it was had not deigned to make itself visible – yet. She was turning back to call to Solavier when a distant cracking as of thunder and stone rolled across the bay from the island.

A chill ran through Alandis' shoulders, not just from the wind. She turned back as it crawled over the island's crest with a seething hiss.

It *was* a dragon. Not just any dragon, but one of the Vanaile, fluid as water and thrice the size of Mother. Sea-pearls and frilled waves crested the skull, its eerie white eyes glowing like a pulsing star. Its wings were crisp like frosted mist, disappearing against the sky, glassy skin like an icy skeleton, translucent enough that the sun cast iridescence across the turbulent waves.

As it looked at Alandis across the bay, clutching at the mossy island of Nan'mier, the tail, edged like a seica, curled about, crushing the third lighthouse that had marked the upper terrace.

Alandis raised her hand towards the creature, letting the amber glow against the sun.

I have called you to the edge of my territory, Vanaile! I hold by the dragon's honor, and I will not harm you. Yet I will do what I have to, to keep you from harming my territory, this island and its mainland, the Salyšalis of my people.

The Vanaile hissed again, tail and talons cracking the stone beneath it as the water dripping from it formed rainbowed waterfalls that spilled over the edge into the sea. Usually, the dragon's honor was enough to get a little breather, but not this time. At least, not that kind of breather.

The Vanaile let out a fierce breath, not of fire, but of pouring, rippling steam, so violent that the water crashed and crested, pounding over the bay to meet the girl on the bank.

A faint shriek sounded from behind Alandis. Once again, the curious children of Isola had assumed they would be safe behind the Dragandrea.

"Lana!" Sol would have pulled her out of the way, but she pushed him back.

"Get the children! *Now!*"

The Zain ran, catching up the children under his arm as Alandis ran into the water, eyes on the barque that still bobbed, desperate to stay afloat.

Better to be on the water where no children were, than on the shore!

The first wave broke around the barque, and Alandis had the sinking feeling that it was only the weakest of the Vanaile's hissy fits. It would have been angry, she was sure, if it had heard that label.

As she pulled herself onto the barque's flooded deck, she heard Sol's desperate call from the shore, but she saw the white eyes in front of her lengthen in a smile. A smile, but not the kind presented at a tea party.

This may be one of my worst unplanned plans yet, Alandis thought.

Solavier and the children froze as the dragon slithered into the water, melting into it. The sea was still.

Still, until it did to Alandis as it had to the barque's cargo.

"Lana. . . *Lana!*"

Sol's breath went unheard as the dragon, barque, and Dragandrea vanished, and the tide rolled back.

Night had fallen. The day had been silent, waiting for Alandis to reappear. She never did. Nor had anything more come out of the sea. The wind had died, as had the rough waves.

Solavier had tried to help mend the damage as was his duty, just as the people tried not to assume the worst. Little was said.

Alandis couldn't hold her breath for more than a minute, Sol knew that. No one dared imagine that the Vanaile had been the first to be unfazed by Alandis – to be against the dragon's honor and kill her – to have drowned her.

Of all the dumbest things she could have done, and yet it wasn't, because the waves hadn't claimed the too-many-children on the shore.

She'd been distracted before they'd even reach the village. Distracted, because of what he'd said? He bit his lip until it bled.

Waiting in a wordless prayer was all Solavier or anyone could do, not daring to frame the thought that nagged – that she was dead.

Further, if Alandis *was* gone, would the dragons leave? Would they overtake all of Lharmeval? And if their last vestige of honor was gone, and the only barrier between them – no one wanted to think that far, either.

Sol did his best to keep his mind awake, not numb. He trusted Alandis, he trusted God, even if he felt he was trusting blindly in this moment. He would keep on, doggedly, until he knew. What would happen then, he wasn't going to try and think of, either.

Sol touched the pommel of his sword. Every night he and Alandis had made a brief patrol of the village. Even if only to keep a sense of normality, he would go; but it would be without the dim glow of the amber. He swung onto Sendoa and let him choose his pace down the slopes.

Sensing his master's mood, it was a slow and steady pace Sendoa set, rhythmic, and the forest was still. The village was quiet, despite the usual passings between homes and closing shops. A dog still barked somewhere, and a kitten pounced across the path before running back, squirrel-like, whence it had come.

Sol could sense the vague relief at the sight of him as he passed through the streets. Some of the children were sitting on their doorsteps, hugging their stuffed animals.

One had a doll modeled after the Dragandrea. It was a silly thing, and it had amused him to no end when such dolls had become commonly made by mothers for their daughters, but now it only hurt. The child must have noticed, because she crept out and handed it up to him.

Sol smiled sadly and tucked the doll under his cloak, wondering again whether Alandis had made it out of the waves. Maybe she'd made it to the island and simply been missed by the scouts or pulled herself out sometime after they'd gone. Or even made it to the farther islands, wherever the Vanaile had been headed. The thought gave him enough hope that he wished it were morning. He'd set out early, if he could be spared, or send out others if he was to be kept on guard.

It was then he realized the child was staring past Sendoa into the dark with frightened eyes as she grabbed at the girth.

The all-too familiar rattle made Solavier sigh as Sendoa shook himself, clearly wanting to be anywhere else but there.

"Alright, did you *really* have to show up tonight? Or do I already know why?"

He motioned for the child to run, and she did, being quickly caught up by her father and taken into the house.

A snort was the reply to Solavier's question as he faced the drake.

"Listen, by now you ought to know some of our language. Alandis isn't here, and the people have all had a day. Would you be polite for once and just . . . I don't know, leave?"

Sendoa seconded the idea.

The drake, already far taller than he had been upon meeting Alandis, wings nearly fully strengthened, shook his moon-fired scales with an angry snort and continued down the road towards him.

"I really don't want to try doing this," Solavier muttered. "Stay with me, Sendoa, I'm going to need you." He glanced at the stars overhead. "And I'm going to need You, too."

He drew his blade, measuring how he might manage to stab the drake's eyes, one of the few fleshy areas on its body. Not enough to kill, certainly, but it might send the drake away for a few days until the sun's energy healed it again.

"Draco. . . what have I told you," a tired voice came from the shadows.

The drake *zipped* happily at the words as its scales fell back into place.

"Alandis?" Solavier leapt from the saddle as the girl slowly stepped out of the shadow of the trees.

She smiled as if she hardly had the strength and, stretching out one hand to hold the drake back, let Sol catch her other hand in his relief.

"I worried we lost you!"

"Very . . . nearly." She dropped her head to his shoulder. She was still drenched, as though she'd only just made it out of the water.

Draco dropped his own head closer to her and breathed out heavily, the warmth nearly drying her at once.

"Thanks, I needed that," Alandis sighed. "Go home, Draco, please don't play tonight."

She pushed his snout away in the direction of the distant mountains, and the drake reluctantly complied, perhaps, for once, out of some sense of compassion. Not that he wouldn't be back on the morrow to excitedly hunt for nonexistent cows in the middle of the village.

Solavier sighed, looking down at Alandis, feeling the weight of all the unthought questions fall back, for now.

"You're in rough shape, Mielė. Let's get you back to the House. You can tell me about everything in the morning, and we'll deal with whatever we need to then. Come on."

He lifted her onto Sendoa and sent the stallion back at a canter, both riders silent.

Solavier took the girl to the doorway of her suite, high on the terraces. He stopped her, just for a moment.

"Alandis, don't do that to me again. If I – If I distracted you – I can't abandon my post, Alandis, but I'll do whatever you need me to."

She shook her head firmly. "It wasn't you, Sol, or the Vanaile. It was me. . . all me."

She didn't say why as she closed the door, but in his heart Solavier began to fear again. He remained on the terrace overlooking the sea for many hours, the moon cresting his hair with silver.

It must be removed, then, she had said, so long ago.

VII

Return of the Dove

Sol was standing once more on the veranda, looking over the sea, when Alandis opened the door and stepped out into the light of the rising sun.

The sky had turned to the rose of crushed grape skins, melded with sparkling pearl, and the clouds, usually stormy, were puffy and swirling breezily like a meringue nearly ready.

The Dragandrea came and stood beside the Zain, seeming – only seeming – to be well, for she stood as straight as ever, and her eyes seemed withdrawn and planning, as usual. Yet her face was paler than Sol had been able to tell in the shadows the night before. For his own part, Solavier was clearly tired.

"You didn't rest," Alandis noted, before he could speak. "Solavier, you ought to have. I know I gave you a hard day yesterday."

"Yes, you did."

"I'm sorry, Sol."

Solavier shook his head, peering into her eyes, biting back the questions that had kept him awake.

"You didn't eat a thing yesterday, I don't think. Come."

He took her then to their accustomed table to haunt, which hung beneath wistful sky-blue and violet wisteria falling from one of the mountain's overhangs. A statue of the holy Lady & Child, guardians of Lharmeval and robed as the Ahren, looked upon Solavier and Alandis lovingly as the pair found the usual spread already waiting.

While food was less affected now than it had been for the first few months, it was still austere, for fruits were usually donated to those who needed them most, leaving coffee, breads, and nut-based concoctions the typical fare. Meat, as was to be expected, had suffered as much as marine fare, and the dragon-terror had made dairy difficult to produce.

Sol didn't touch the harvest nutbreads, or even the roasted tomatoes on rye, only watched Alandis gravely as she endeavored to eat. The growing silence and the worry in her own mind soon forced her to abandon the meal. She put down her fork and finally met his gaze.

"What happened yesterday? Why did the Vanaile take you?"

Alandis leaned her arms on the table and braced her head as though feeling the weight of the water on her shoulders again. She ignored the latter question.

"After the Vanaile took me, it headed north. I could still breathe a little, and eventually I was able to free myself – I don't know if I convinced it to let go or if it didn't particularly notice, but I came up nearer the northern shores of Tryshek, which you know are impassable due to the landslides the tzaidra have created from their lightning storms, and had to alternately swim and walk all the way back."

Solavier stared at her, waiting.

"That was a shorter answer than I was expecting," he prodded at last. "Alandis, what madness possessed you to enter the water like that? *Why?*"

Alandis was at a loss for words, and so Sol questioned her gravely with growing severity. Each question came with unsatisfactory and evasive answers.

Roundabouts exhausted, Solavier gave up.

"What did you mean when you said it wasn't the Vanaile or myself?"

He saw the flinch that she tried to hide.

"You put yourself too close – you know the danger of damaging your implant."

A moment passed with only the distant, running footsteps of Cole and the horses trotting to and from the stables. A blackbird sang overhead and dropped a blossom down onto Alandis' shoulder.

". . . Did you try to kill yourself?"

He asked it so low that it was nearly blown away by the wind, and of that there was little.

Alandis drew a shaky breath. All the strength that was her built-up shell peeled back to reveal the self she'd been doing her best to mask, and Sol wanted to cry.

"Alandis, Alandis! I was there the day you thought the implant should be removed!"

"I – I don't know, I don't know if I gave in," she breathed helplessly. "I – was punishing myself for everything, as I always have been since I left Erevale."

Solavier numbly sank down in front of her.

"Alandis. . ." the grief in his eyes pierced her. She covered her face, any trace of the Dragandrea gone.

"Alandis, I triggered this! Don't let me do this to you!"

"No, no, I told you it wasn't you!" Alandis raised her head again. "No, Sol, don't – don't hurt yourself! I never told you what I've been going through, I was so – lost!"

"Mielė, little Dove, you don't have to be lost!" He gripped her hands, which now seemed so oddly out of place against the vambraces she wore. "Tell me, let me help you. I'll listen and I'll be here even if no one else is. You know everyone who loves you *would* be here if you let them – Trys, Enara, your family."

He watched as Alandis became again the girl from Erevale, sweet and gentle and anxious under his stress, as the fears came tumbling out, repeating again her terrors of the implant, of the dragons being her fault, of not being able to cast them out permanently, and of running away. She feared, too, of failing and losing lives besides her own, and she feared the Vanaile.

"The Vanaile's fluidity answered to my suicidal thoughts and tried to solve my problem by drowning me, and its watery nature means it's a flip of a coin whether it wants to listen to anything else! The Vanaile is the most dangerous of the dragons we've met," she said with a shiver. "It did still have the dragon's honor – but it would seem the dragon's honor includes killing another dragon if the second so wishes."

"An evil thing," Solavier muttered.

"I don't know – how to protect against it again. Part of me thought that if I wasn't here, the dragons would leave. I know that isn't true."

Hugging herself, Alandis looked away.

"I know that I'm the only one who can help against them, even if they came because of the amber in my heart. If I fail, I fail Lharmeval, and Lharmeval will fall to them. Please, don't let me fail, Sol!"

"We'll find a way, Alandis. I promise. I promise, as I promise that I won't let you lose yourself again. You mustn't choose to drown. Regardless of whether the amber is at fault, God has given you the task and grace to hold the dragons back from harming Lharmeval, and I, if it be in my power, will hold your own dragons back from you."

He glanced up at the statue of the Lady as he drew something from his pocket and put it in Alandis' hands. It was an icon, the travel-diptych style, wrapt in rose velvet marked with amber stones. Inside nestled two portraits, one of the Lady and Child, and one of the Healing Death.

Tears pricked Alandis' eyes.

"This is my mother's favorite image," she told him, touching the golden halos of the Lady with her fingertips. "You remembered I mentioned that?"

"I did. Since you won't tell her where you are, this is so you can keep your other Mother close. She was strong like you, even with the sorrow that no one else could know."

Alandis nodded and looked up at him. He saw the smile reappear on her face, but it wasn't because of the icon.

"What?"

She nodded towards the doll he'd forgotten, tucked into his belt beneath his cloak.

"I thought you found those amusing."

He drew it out with a faint smile and shook his head.

"One of the children handed her – you – it, to me last night when I thought I'd lost you."

Alandis' eyes softened and she stood. "I'm sorry, Sol! I'm here now."

The Zain nodded, drawing himself up at the remembrance that she was, in fact, safe now. Safe, and the Dragandrea was returning as he watched.

"We'll return it when we go into the village to take stock of the damage," Solavier said, and now he, too, smiled. He stood and stretched out his hand to her.

"Alandis . . . I need you to trust me. I'm going to hold on to you in that I won't let you hurt yourself. Please, trust my judgment – especially in the event that I'm left to handle things again. I'll do the best I can, but I hope you'll never take temporary leave again."

"I trust you, Sol."

Solavier sighed and glanced out again over the cliffside. The water was turning from indigo to lavender, and the sky was filling with gold streams of cirrus clouds, tinted rainbow hues as the sun struck the ice within them. It was peaceful, but for how long? When would the next dragon strike? If it did, would the Dragandrea meet it, or the Dove?

"Isn't today the day you write to your family? Why don't we take care of that? Write the note, and I'll take it down to the aviary and send it off for you."

He didn't disclose his reason for asking for her trust. There may have been many, but there was one imminent – to put his own hand to that note and rewrite the story of her isolation. Whether she liked it or not, her family would come. He knew now a taste of what they must have felt at Alandis' leaving and her reticence.

Some time later, Alandis turned her head aside from writing the note, ceasing the scratching of quill on parchment. Solavier had been standing still, listening to the quiet of the morning.

"Do you hear?" Alandis asked softly.

"What?"

"The doves. They've returned."

Solavier caught his breath.

Faintly came that mournful call, so familiar even after many months, for Alandis had filled the gap with the hymn she would sing when she thought she was alone.

"So, they have."

"We haven't had a thunderstorm in weeks," Alandis mused. "The wind has been less, too. The dragons have grown reticent."

"They tire, then."

"I don't know," Alandis answered slowly. "I don't know, Sol. I don't."

VIII

Releasing the Dove

With the return of the doves came a relative peace, reflected in the dusting of sunlit snow that was Lharmeval's winter. It now sugared the leaves of every tree and the petal of every flower, as frost marbled the ground.

Life was likewise turning to a relative normal. Normal, until someone showed up, the kind of someone who hung on the fringe, like a half-acknowledged shadow, invisible until suddenly he was there, and no one knew how he hadn't been seen.

He was a knight from Marén, the mainland to the southeast, the country Lharmeval was content to be away from. His armor was the rusted black verdigris of crucible steel and coppered bronze, stabbed with an engraving of a writhing snake, ebony fangs bared.

He was a black knight, true to legends, yet he watched with a silent passiveness. Passive yet disturbing as his eyes followed Alandis about her work, and somehow, every time she turned from a dragon, he was there in the distance on a ridge, black horse and all. The scythe on his back marked the clouds with its silhouette, like a talon against a tattered pennant.

Disturbed, since there was no information on him and nothing to be said, Alandis ignored him, a skill she'd only recently acquired.

Solavier, however, did not, and made a point of blocking the knight's view even from a distance; the Zain found that whenever he rode towards the knight, the mysterious rider would make his exeunt, albeit without running.

With disgust, the Ahren heard him singing songs of bloodshed as he rode through the trees alone, the kind of song forbidden among the people of Lharmeval, but they were loath to try to cease his voice, for he was tall and far too strong of build, and thickly plated by dragon-skin and armor.

It was two weeks after the incident with the Vanaile when Alandis finally had a breather to take stock of the damage for restitution. She knew Solavier was likely already with the horses as she slammed the aschura writing case closed, capped the little enameled pen, and shooed the dove out the window, with one last try.

Just one more time.

She bent her head a moment as the amber fluttered painfully, recalling the day of the doves so long ago. Now that the doves had returned, the next sunrise would see another group of doves released, the first since that spring. There would be no Trys to hurt this time. There was, however, a Solavier, and the fear of causing some form of repeat weighed on her.

Why the doves had returned was still a mystery – the skies had been oddly quiet, with only occasional forays from Draco and Mother. Wind was irregular, but the shadows seemed oddly deep.

The dove drew Alandis back from her thoughts as it chirped, fluttering anxiously, and darted away from the balcony around toward the back of the House. The doves *always* flew straight to the west when she released them.

Alandis jerked the door of her suite open with the distinctive sense that there was someone waiting for her. As suspected, it wasn't Solavier.

"I wondered when you'd show up. So, who are you?" she asked, as the door slammed behind her.

The knight moved languidly from the side of the alcove, where he'd stood in the shadows.

"Dlam U'Dell. Like you, I'm here to fight the dragons."

"I'm not here to fight the dragons, I'm here to protect the people."

"Same thing."

"No, they're vastly different. You're here for the dragons; I'm here for the people. I fight the dragons, but they know I won't harm them, so they respect me. You, on the other hand, appear to mean business –" she looked at the scythe. "The more fear you put into them, the less they'll listen to me, and they can choose to override any fight put against them."

"You sound as though you *like* dragons."

"I dislike dragons as I dislike rain – they're beautiful but sometimes a disturbance as the season goes. I don't choose to be a destroyer."

"My Lady Adrastĕja!"

Solavier's voice was sharp as he hailed from the path crossing over the veranda and approached.

He condescended to drop a single glance on the intruder and took Alandis' arm.

"We're needed in the village, Dragandrea. As for you," he said to U'Dell without bothering to learn his name, "you'd do better not to hang around private doorways unannounced. It might call a dragon down on your head . . . so to speak."

He pulled Alandis aside and whispered the news to her. More omens were floating in from sea: broken ships, not only of Lharmeval, but also of the islands.

Chills struck through Alandis' heart. She strove not to show it, though she reached for Sol's hand, and they rode down to the village to hold council and take stock for restitution.

No survivors had been found, they were told, but given the ships' paths inland, they could easily have been picked up elsewhere along the coastline or among the islands. Alandis prayed that this was the case. Until they knew, all that could be done was to focus on receipt-making.

With an outward peace she didn't feel, she called anyone forward whose livelihoods had sustained damage.

The man whose barque had been crushed by the Vanaile's attack pushed his way ahead of the others and chose to take it out on Alandis, regardless of any gratitude he'd had previously for her protection.

Alandis listened patiently against his tirade, and when he had finished, spoke.

"I understand that though you know that if we had done otherwise, the dragon may have killed all, you need an outlet for all of this. Please, write out a receipt of all it cost you, and I will send it to the council in Erenni so that they might gauge what might be done for you."

The man settled down, quieted at her understanding, and did as she asked. Many more followed, some wrongfully, writing false charges out of greed, but many were the ones who knew the truth of these receipts and that they could be discarded.

The black knight came and dropped his hands on the edge of the table, leaning over her.

"And how many lives have been lost, Dragandrea? How will you pay for those?"

Alandis stopped.

"We do not know, U'Dell. They cannot be repaid, and while there may not have been a great many, even one was too much."

"Then kill the dragons. If you won't –" He straightened and faced the people gathered about. "I will! In Marén, we fear not the unconquerable dragons. I will be your dragon-fighter so that you will not suffer again!"

Solavier grabbed the man's shoulder and forced him into the nearest seat.

"Move against the dragons, and you'll make a mess for the entire kingdom. Wait in patience and mind your tongue. The Dragandrea has been given her title by the people, and it cannot be taken away."

Alandis touched Sol's arm and turned to Dlam U'Dell.

"Dragons have a strange sense of propriety. They know I can't kill them, but they will accept my tenacity against them as any dragon would. As far as they are concerned, I *am* a dragon and this *is* my territory."

She stood.

"I will defend it as best I can, and these dragons will not spread to the rest of Lharmeval. If that is why it has been quiet of late, I will find them. Tomorrow after the releasing of the doves, I hunt for the dragons in their own territory, particularly that of the Vanaile. Solavier will remain here to defend from any wyrms that may arrive in my absence. You, U'Dell, may remain here, but don't raise your weapons against anything unless given leave by Solavier."

"We'll need to discuss this further," Solavier replied. His eyes sparked a warning.

"Agreed."

As soon as U'Dell would let them pass, Solavier pulled Alandis outside into the icy blue of the snowflake-blooms. Sissi and Sendoa were in the garden behind the longhouse, pawing aside the snow to reach the sweet crimson roots of the blossoms.

"Alandis, what are you thinking?" Solavier charged reproachfully. "After what you did the first time we met the Vanaile, I can't leave you alone again. Besides, you told me yourself you wouldn't know how to fight it a second time. Just how do you expect me to protect from dragons in your absence? Raising my sword against them will do little! I couldn't have held back even the drake by blade alone, not for long."

"It's not so problematic." Alandis patiently dusted snow from Sissi's shoulders. "You must remember that the dragons have been scarcely seen besides the effects of the Vanaile, and they will be drawn to my movement. I don't believe you shall have any trouble while I'm away. You always have clever ideas when I need you, Sol," she reminded him. "I trust you."

"Clever like releasing that barque that you then decided to jump on? I'm not sure about that," Solavier snorted.

"Sol. . .regardless of my own decision, that was necessary. There's the time you lured the firedrakes into the lake during the tzaidra's thunderstorms, and got both pairs half-shocked into sleep, or when you drew the swamp wyrms into quicksand –"

"Funny how often I lure them with food," Sol replied darkly, "and we don't have enough of that to play with anymore."

"Sol . . . you asked me to trust you. I do trust you. Trust yourself. I know you can't speak to dragons, I know you can't kill them, but I know that you can protect from them, and that the dragons have respect for you. They've told me so, in case I've never told you."

"What?"

"They call you the 'Anbaerra-gaerattza,' usually the 'Anbaerr-èskalak."

She smiled as he translated that into their own language. A little smile started, met by Alandis', for

Solavier was, indeed, the "amber's whetstone", or more specifically to the dragons, the amber's scales.

Just as he pulled her out of her own dragons' mouths, he was her only way to keep fighting the dragons; and just as the only material sharp enough to strengthen a dragon's claws were its own scales, he was the only one strong enough to strengthen her.

"Well enough, then," he surrendered, "but you haven't answered the first of my questions."

"I'll make every promise that I can to not risk throwing away my life."

"Yet you tell me you aren't certain you were fully of your own mind the first time. Alandis, that's not helping."

"You can't leave U'Dell to his own devices," Alandis reminded him. "You can't come with me, Sol."

He exhaled as he warmed Sendoa's nose, by now covered with snow and icing-over nectar.

"Promise me for my sake, then, that you won't make me believe it was my fault."

Alandis laid her gloved hand on his face, and the wounded look softened.

"I promise, Sol."

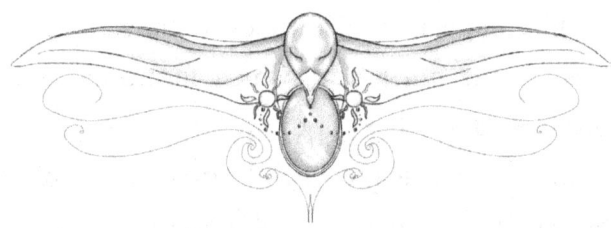

The following morning dawned the coldest yet, the air shivering with silver and pearl, and the sun shone like a watered reflection through misty clouds that bode of another dappling of snow.

Alandis' eyes picked out all the discrepancies between the Erevale tradition and the Ahren.

There were no tents, but carved canopies, lightweight that sprang open and closed at will like a string of paper snowflakes. White doves were nowhere to be seen within the violet, ivied cages, for they would be lost against the snow; instead, feathers of glaucous haze and misty cameo-rose glinted between the leaves.

Christmas roses were twined in wreaths of wisteria-wood and berries, and the icy sparkling of winter forget-me-nots was strewn everywhere, tied with twine and ribbons of rose. Winter aconite popped through the ice with the buttery gold of a sunrise, crushing underfoot as Alandis and Solavier made their way across the meadow to the star-hung birches on the other side, which formed a wall against the sea-wind.

While the people grew lighthearted once more, there was an undercurrent of unease as U'Dell stomped his way through the snow amid the gathering, and the thoughts of doubt which he had introduced still flitted through everyone's minds.

Alandis had found a perch in the low branches of one of the birches, from whence she was content to watch, fingers stroking the crucifix ever slung at her side. Sol occupied himself with shifting back and forth behind the icicles, letting them distort his view of U'Dell.

Alandis was humming the Dove's song under her breath, and by the trembling of the amber's glow, which she kept instinctively covering, Solavier knew she was still struggling. He released U'Dell from his study.

"What's wrong, Alandis?"

She shook her head without glancing at him, gazing at the sky.

"I need to keep the dragons on my mind and nothing else."

"Alandis. There are dragons within you, too. What dragons are you fighting now?"

"U'Dell. . . the Vanaile. . . but mostly Trys. The sky always makes me think of him, when it's all blue and gold," she murmured. She beat her hand against the branch, knocking snow down onto Sol's shoulder.

"I'm so confused! He's never tried to contact me, not once! I think you and my family are all wrong that he would come for me. He cares, but not *that* much."

"If he knows why you ran away, as the Ahren seem to sense such things even if he was not told, it's possible he shies from coming after you, fearing that he'll make it worse and possibly repel you further."

Alandis dropped her head against the birch.

"I didn't want you to say that," she groaned. "It doesn't help, Sol –"

"For goodness' sakes, why have you never contacted him, then?"

"I tried! I tried," she faltered. "Each time there was no reply, but I was never quite sure where he was; whether at home in Erevale or on shoring duties in any number of places along the coast. I sent a last note yesterday. If there's no reply, I won't try again."

"Well. Then . . . could he possibly not be receiving them? The doves may simply have missed him. Besides, with the wind so common in our kingdom now, they could easily be blown off course."

"I want a yes or a no! I don't want to think of the might haves or ifs at this point. I'm so confused, I'm so scared to let go even though I logically think I ought to – if the voice in my head wasn't true, so many other things might only be sand – he's been my anchor," she finished miserably. "That voice always says to love him as God loves me. I – counted on him for so long, I've loved him since I met him–"

She found Sol giving her a side-hug, the way Ean and Trys always did.

"Perhaps, Alandis, it's to love even if Trys isn't choosing to be with you; as the first bride rejected God and lost its place to the second. Yet, He still loves the first and waits patiently for it to turn. I don't say this in my own favor, only that there may be more to that call than simple confusion."

"I know you realize Trys shouldn't be your anchor, and I know you fear these other promises that may tumble down if you remove what you've built on your love for him, but it's alright to let go. It's alright not to feel alright, to drift and to find a different shore. It doesn't mean you forget the harbor you came from, only that maybe you followed a Star lesser than the Northern."

"It doesn't mean not to love him, but to be willing to release him, so that both of you can fulfill whatever Deo's will is. It doesn't mean that Trys will never come for you; it doesn't mean that you're lost if he doesn't come, because you can always go to him, and if he isn't waiting, I'm here; and if I'm not the one, then there will be someone else. I promise you, you aren't lost, even if you wander."

"It's – alright?"

"It's alright." He held her hand, curled tightly around the crucifix.

"I . . . have been afraid that I would hurt you today, the way I hurt Trys at the last releasing."

Sol's eyes smiled gently.

"You haven't, and if you did ever, remember: I'll never force you, nor will I run away."

A call went up, and with it, the music paused. A cloud of misty moonlight wings fluttered into the trees, swarming for a minute, bobbing as it considered a flight to the west.

"Here," Solavier said, and lifted a last cage that had been settled in the snow. A lone dove, far too small and iridescent, nestled inside.

"They gave me this one, the handlers," he explained. "She was the odd one out of her group, and even doves sometimes can be cruel. She's yours to keep . . . or to release."

Slowly Alandis took the cage from him, and hanging it on the bough beside her, unlatched the door and took the nestling dove in her hands.

Her breath shivered on the air for a space, in time with the amber; then she let go.

The dove hesitated. It was only for a moment, until two glaucous doves, as small as she, called her up into the branches. Alandis looked to her empty hands and a sigh escaped her lips.

"I . . . feel I'm seeing things for the first time and I'm frightened," she admitted. "I don't know if I've truly let go. Yet . . . it feels good, to release him, for I worried so that I had hurt him and that I'd been inappropriate and too hard!"

She hesitantly looked at him as he took the now-empty and chilled hands in his.

"I guess –" she began, uncertainly.

"Don't rush into it, Alandis. This wasn't for my gain. Take the time to love yourself the way you haven't been able to with this weight. Keep choosing to let go, but if God makes it clear that He wants you to be with Trys, then you'll know."

He pressed her hand and withdrew as she smiled, at once like the Dove, and yet not – a trifle lighter, if more vulnerable.

If the Adrastėjas contacted Trys, would he come? Sol mulled, uncertain whether Trys' arrival would overjoy Alandis, send her scrambling after a dragon, or precipitating herself into the sea a second time. That was one reason he didn't want to let her go after the Vanaile alone.

It was nearing noon when Solavier rode with the Dragandrea to the ridge and reluctantly took his leave of her. He agreed to stay behind to watch U'Dell, but only if Alandis gave every possible promise not to lose herself.

"I fear he will make his intentions against the dragons good," Alandis said. "That's one reason I need you to stay. He'll bring fire down on Lharmeval if he tries anything."

She glanced up at the sky, which still showed no sign of storm.

With a little smile, she added, "I expect you wouldn't stay behind if he follows me."

"He'd better not follow," Sol growled, then paused, twisted. "At least if he did, I'd be able to keep watch over you."

He watched snowflakes pearling on Alandis' hair for a minute.

"You're sure you know where you're going?"

"Verily. Close enough, at least. The Vanaile resides somewhere in the glacial seas."

"That might have been a trap for it to tell you so. Lana, please –"

"Dearest Èskalak, you've already rethought it with me. I've got to stop the Vanaile! We've likely lost too many lives because of its attack on the ships. I've got to convince it somehow."

What that somehow might be, she had no idea, and Solavier's brow was creased fit to remain so. Alandis put her frozen fingers against the marks.

"I have the Lady Maia and her Son, Scier, with me," she reminded him, drawing on the bravery she wasn't feeling. "There will be a way. Keep U'Dell from making matters worse."

She was pulling Sissi away when Solavier put his hands on the reins.

"The last time I said this, it made it worse, Alandis. But I cherish you, and I pray that this time, it makes you think twice before you let anything draw you to your death. If you need to fly, know that I will always be your safe place to land."

He stooped and kissed her hand. Alandis reached up and hugged him for a moment.

"I shouldn't be letting you go," Solavier groaned softly as the girl turned away. "I shouldn't!"

"It can't be helped right now, Sol. I need you to let me go and trust that I can fly, at least once."

"Deo keep you, little Dove!"

Alandis squeezed his hand and left the Zain there, watching as the Dragandrea disappeared across the snowy plains.

IX

Eyes in the Ice

They'd told her if she lost it, she'd be broken forever. . .

"They will come for you. One cannot choose suicide!"

"How many lives have been lost, Dragandrea? How will you pay for those?"

"Think twice before you let anything draw you to your death. . . shouldn't let you go!"

Alandis could hear the voices swirling in her mind like the snowflakes whirling on the wind. She shivered, drawing the pearly, mink-lined velvet cloak closer. She had clasped it with a dove-shaped brooch that Solavier had carved for her, but it clacked against the amber that alone seemed to remain warm in the chill.

Crossing the snowy plateaus, Alandis had left Tryshek now and traversed Nvilna, making camp twice. The northern territory was unfamiliar to her, except by hearsay. She had no idea whether there were ice dragons, too, and jumped at every shifting shape of snow. She shook her head at her imagination.

The voices in the wind and snow were surely also her imagination. Echoes of warnings, they reminded her that somehow she'd escaped damage to the amber, but would she remain so lucky?

She remembered, too, the haunted gaze Sol had held every time he worried about her departure.

"Maia! Help me keep my promise?"

Alandis cracked open the diptych she'd carried in her purse and prayed that she wouldn't hurt Solavier worse than she had hurt Trys.

How was Solavier faring? Was her hunch of the dragons correct, and his hands were full only with holding back U'Dell?

Once she had thrown a glance over her shoulder and thought she spied a dark figure on horseback in the distance, watching, but it was only a speck against the whiteness, and she couldn't be sure. Besides, while this was not the most hospitable place to be traveling in the winter, there would be plenty of others on the roads.

Alandis pressed onward and rounded the glacial bay of Tèsseré. A glacier, dripping blue-gold in the morning, slipped down the mountains to the west.

She could hear the cracking as the calvings come raining down into the water.

There was no sight of the Vanaile, but she had a creeping feeling that this was, in fact, where she was headed.

Leaving Sissi, Alandis alternately slid and crunched her way across the frost-encased foliage to the water's edge.

A large iceberg, seemingly rooted to the center of the bay, dominated the horizon. With color shifts from white to crystal blue and turquoise, the dome of the iceberg was shattered into sharp pinnacles like a scream, deceptively showered by the recent snow. Archways and grand, mawing corridors led inside, the misted sunlight reverberating like phosphorescence. The outer walls were carved and scratched in vibrant blue stripes, eerily claw-like.

Smaller ice floes and growlers bumped around its foot, until the bay appeared like chips of ice slushed together with the blue of pansies, forget-me-nots, cornflowers, and starflowers, which was a favored delicacy in these northern regions. Now Alandis could see where the inspiration had come from.

With no sign of dragon or destruction, Alandis rested her eyes on the water peacefully lapping at her feet, thinking heavily of the damaged ships – of all the dragons – of home.

"Where are you," she sighed. "Deo. . . I'm so tired."

As she picked out the glassy stones littering the shallows, she began to realize that there was something else hiding in her reflection. A shock sent her nerves shrieking when it hit her that the eyes staring back at her were not her own, but the ghostly white of the Vanaile.

She stumbled backwards, thinking she was now seeing things again, but no, the water foamed and shapeshifted, yet rather than dragging her in, as if sensing her change of thought, it rocketed through the water towards the iceberg.

"Wait!"

Alandis followed as best as she could, hopping across the ice floes. There were many tunnels driving their way into the ice. One, two, three, were only shallow and abruptly curved around to the entrance.

Was there an entrance underwater? That must have been how the Vanaile entered. She hesitated, debating the danger of trying to find it in freezing water, versus not stopping the Vanaile. She knew what Sol would say, and flinched, remembering her promise.

Momentarily helpless, she held her breath to think. No, there *had* to be a way in from the outside, but it would be as difficult as a frozen dive.

Her hair, having been loosely netted by a weave of slender braids to lay warmly against her neck, she now caught up into a ponytail. Setting her seica to the ice, she began to claw her way up the iceberg, using the scraped lines and her seica to find footholds. Near the summit, hidden by crystal talons and spires, was a fifty-degree slope down into the iceberg's depths – or so she hoped.

Or did she hope?

The chill was biting at her, despite the amber's warmth.

Don't do it, she seemed to hear Sol say, but could it be helped?

She perched there for some time, staring at the sunrise. All the things she had done – all the times she had sustained some injury – paled in comparison to her reckless facing of the Vanaile the first time.

Was she in full control? She had been seeing things already; how did she know she hadn't built a wall to tell herself this was right?

She felt that she was wobbling back and forth over an edge, trying to draw on two reins that pulled her back from the thoughts she was plunging into, but her strength was too far gone.

She saw herself within the heart of a vortex, with no knowledge of where to turn, for everything was spinning: everything was there, and nothing was.

It was the feeling that she was broken down and would never be fulfilled, nothing would prove her, nothing would hold back the dragons, everything she did was a failure – her skill with the dragons had only brought death.

Sol loved a shadow and a ghost, and that was why Trys had turned away – he had seen the shell that was the Dove, the facade behind which was nothing but fear.

"No," she said aloud, dazedly shaking her head. Whether or not all that was true, there were two things that she did know for certain: both men would perish those thoughts from her mind, and while neither would approve of her dropping into a dragon's lair, what else *could* she do?

Alandis sighed, taking out a flask to check that it was empty. She watched the last few drops of coffee sink into the snow. It had been nice to have the hot drink the first day, but now she was regretting not saving enough to wake up her chilled mind. At least Solavier had thought to give it to her, because coffee had been, unusually, the furthest thing from her mind.

Alandis groaned. There was no one else there to tell her what she was thinking, what her secret reasons were.

She watched the sliding shadows. Even in the morning light they were spectrally deep, as they had been in Isola. Was that merely her imagination, too?

The northwestern sky was still in a deep haze, deep enough that the stars peeked through; the King's star, that of Scier, glimmered; overhead, the triangle of the archangels; and in the south, Maia's constellation held the sky captured. Even once they vanished, they would still be there, just as they were when she never felt them.

"Help me keep my promise, end this without ending me, for Sol's sake and my family's!"

Alandis sheathed her seica and slipped down the slope.

Four seconds of sliding found a vertical wall of ice rushing up through the shadows to meet her dark-struck eyes – she barely turned her shoulder to it in time to save her head. Her shoulder slammed into the ice and sent shivers rattling through the nerves in her arm.

"*Not* my best idea," Alandis muttered, as her vision wobbled a moment. She gained a foothold after a few near-slides and began to prowl the tunnel.

The light here was dim but spoke of the bright turquoise bands of dusk. She was grateful for the warmth and the ebb and flow of the amber's light, though she grew hyperaware of its consistent pulse and the desire to tear it out.

She clenched her fist to keep her promise and kept moving.

Creeping through the ice and echoing off the walls was the rolling, gurgling sound of the waves that sloshed beneath her feet, and groans and cracks of ice as it warmed in the sun, and the saltwater froze within its veins. The musical plinking of the occasional droplet beat a static pace for Alandis' steps as she came to the first branching of the iceberg.

There was a strange peace here, leaving Alandis feeling that she could have left her breath hanging to rest. She was certain that the Vanaile was aware she had followed it. If it could shapeshift into water, it was equally likely it could shapeshift into ice. She could have been treading on its tail at that moment, for all she knew.

The thought made her hesitate to place her next step as her eyes roved around the walls. The listlessly shimmering light played further tricks on her eyes.

She shook her head and slipped to the branching-off of the corridor. The cracked ice broke into a cavern, littered with pillars. There was evidence of scale-sharpening on the far walls, and several pillars had been sliced through the abdomen, as though by a carelessly-swung tail.

Her breath shivered. The crisp crackling ran around the cavern walls behind her back, chittering like the laughing of many watching eyes.

She was going to die.

The wave of despair returned, crashing over her shoulders.

Trapped in the sinking ghost of her fears, the iceberg rested in her stomach, taking over her insides until she was more chilled inside than out, and the amber felt like fire against it. She started to pull at the implant and scarcely stopped, grasping at the ridges of ice around her instead.

Sol's suspicions were right, she had thrown herself headfirst into that iceberg without truly discerning what she was doing.

Whether her family would have to see her blood on the ice, or Sol, or Trys –

But it wasn't Trys she thought of first; it wasn't the thought that always had come before, of the way Trys shielded her from the wind, and the longing for that shelter now.

It was Sol. It was *Sol* whom she wanted to appear at her shoulder to face the Vanaile with her.

She imagined his face, remembering the way relief had broken over it when she'd stepped from the shadows after her near-drowning; the agony, too, when they'd both realized what she had done.

She didn't want that to be etched on his face again.

She was supposed to be the Dragandrea, not the Dove. She was *asked* to be the Dragandrea and keep the Dove from flying at every thought. She wrapped her fingers around the crucifix. The iceberg inside began to melt, just a little, until it no longer froze her stomach solid.

The Vanaile was not rushing to meet her. Whether it was a trap or not, she had the time to speak.

Alandis stepped into the cavern. The crackling fell silent as she cast the amber's voice across the room.

I have left my territory to find you, Vanaile. I am not here to harm you, but those who follow in my footsteps will hunt you for what you have done. Give your word that you will not destroy our people, and I will hold them back.

The ice seemed to fizz before her eyes like wreathing steam, until those eerie eyes were flashing into hers.

X

Heart of Ice

"So much for waking up my chilled mind!" Alandis muttered, wincing as she skidded into another wall.

She was running through a near hall of mirrors, where the ice fractured like the face of obsidian struck, shining like glass. The Vanaile was hard to see among its favored setting, glassy as it was itself, but every time it hurled steam at her, the walls began to melt.

Without deigning to speak a word to the amber, the Vanaile had instigated a slipping, sliding chase from top to bottom of the iceberg, seemingly pleased with every bruise Alandis bore from crashing into the ice.

That the Vanaile truly wanted to kill her was not what she had thought she'd face. It had been a trap, as Solavier had feared!

He shouldn't have let me go – no! It's not his fault–

She cried out as a searing sensation ripped at her left arm and neck as a shot of steam encased the entire room in fog, after scoring a direct hit on her skin. Blistering pain seemed to stick to the freshly dampened fabric of her blouse.

She grit her teeth and fumbled for the wall to guide her. She couldn't see a thing and couldn't hear anything save her ragged breath and the *plish-plosh* of ice turning to slush.

Feeling about blindly, she located the source of the sound, scooped up some of the melting ice for her burn, and ducked again as a rattling intake of breath warned her of another vent coming.

"Don't you want to stop wrecking your lair?" Alandis cried in exasperation, but the answer was clearly *no*.

The ice cracked and rained down on her. She blocked it from striking her head, cleaving it with her seica.

Another crash, and without sight of the falling ice this time, the path was obstructed, leaving only a narrow gap near the roof. It seemed loose enough that her seica could have hacked a way through, but she couldn't risk that pile of ice being the Vanaile in disguise.

Equally, she couldn't risk standing still, regardless of the true identity of the near avalanche sliding down the path behind her.

She grit her teeth and leapt for a handhold, flinging herself through the gap with hardly a breath to spare. The Vanaile smote the ice aside and tore after her.

Ahead was a sea-level entrance to the iceberg's chambers, the now-storming sea licking at the ice as it abruptly broke away.

Alandis slid to a stop, grasping at the clefts in the wall to keep from sliding into the ocean at her feet.

Jaws gaping wide, the Vanaile snaked its head at her, who-knows-how-many tons of dragon-flesh and water ready to crush her.

What had she said about not diving? It was either the frozen ocean or the dragon, and either way would not stop the Vanaile's attacks on Lharmeval's people.

Maia! Scier!

The Vanaile froze, talons locked in the ice, and cocked its head. For a moment, the breath of both hung in the air, one a net of frost, one of steam, and with one thought of whether that name was known even to the dragons.

Alandis exhaled.

"You've made your point, Vanaile. This is your territory, and I am an invader; just as you invaded mine."

The dragon seemed torn between hissing and confusion; scratching its claws on the ice, it ruffled its wings and frill before deigning to sit, for all the world like a puppy at attention.

Alandis' fingers slowly loosened from their lock on the crucifix.

"I know I am not dragon-born, and the dragon-blood within me is illicit to you; yet it keeps me alive, as it does you. I have worked to protect both our peoples: I ask you to grant me the honor of the dragons. Now, for the sake of Scier and His Mother, tell me of the shipwrecks."

Warily, wreaths of cooling steam ringing its head, it snorted in icy laughter and lowered its eyes to stare into hers.

You do not ask why I would have killed you, or why I told you where to find me? One ice-heart to another, I drew you here, testing whether you actually wanted to die; you did, but at least you had the sense to run. I am not like my kindred, I am not willing to heed you, but I am willing to explain my wrath!

I starved, for the waters have been growing emptied by our presence, and the sunlight in my veins prefers to sleep; but you've earned their destruction, for I can feel my kindred dragons dying! What would you expect of me but to tear my claws into your holdings?

It snapped its teeth inches from her face.

What has been done to my kindred, human dragon? What have you done with them?

"What do you mean? I've hardly seen the other dragons of late – You feel the dragons dying?"

It laughed dryly, coiling its tail slitheringly around itself.

You know you can only understand me, and vice versa, because of the amber. All dragons are connected by the amber in their veins, so no, dragons do not normally kill each other, even at request, as I nearly killed you . . . human dragon.

You ask for the dragon's honor – I have sensed the demise of the others! All I possess is the knowledge that humans must have caused it in some way!

Answer to me, ice-heart! What will you do now, and shall I kill you? Even you have seen the shadows growing long and felt their pain.

The tail thrashed, dangerously close to flicking Alandis into the water.

She didn't notice.

A rampant chill negated the burning in her neck and shoulder as she began to realize the implications of the Vanaile's words: the shadows that had seemed far too deep and long – was that why her heart had ached physically, and not because of the trouble over Trys and Solavier?

"This is why you were willing to drown me?" she breathed, turning her eyes back to the Vanaile's face.

Yes, I intend to punish you for causing the death of the dragons! By holding them back in your protection, you're allowing them to be killed –

"So! You are, indeed, a friend of dragons!" a voice rang out as a figure stooped through the passage.

U'Dell had found his way inside, sharp-edged armor and all, unfazed by the hulking bulk of the Vanaile. Alandis' heart thudded against the amber and she looked for Solavier. He didn't appear.

"Far more proper would it be, I deem," U'Dell sneered, "to call you *Dragaidorea* than Dragandrea! The question of the lady, or the traitor—"

"U'Dell—!" Alandis warned.

The Vanaile hissed and shot forward to presumably flatten the black knight, but Alandis slapped her hand against the dragon's forearm.

"He can't hurt you!" she reminded the Vanaile. "Please, let me handle him."

She turned her back on the dragon.

"U'Dell, what *are* you doing here?" Alandis demanded, stalling while she waited for Sol's inevitable, if late, apparition.

Dlam moved languidly forward, testing the scythe's blade against the back of his gauntlet.

"I'm here to kill the dragon, of course; I followed you."

At which saying, the Vanaile arched its back and wings like a cat, and Alandis had to pray it would stay back as she pressed her arm against its rattling scales.

U'Dell must have been on her trail the entire time for the snow not to have settled in Sissi's tracks. Would Solavier have been torn between dealing with U'Dell and an unexpected attack?

She felt her breath grow shallow and her vision sparked purple and green for a minute as her eyes darted to the entrance again. She shook her head to clear it.

"Dlam, it has no weakness! You can't kill it, but it *can* kill you. I'd advise you to come no closer."

"Nonsense."

Still, Dlam halted two yards from her.

"It has a weakness, *my lady*, one you've chosen not to use well: one reason why this is a man's job, not a maiden's. I know what grace the dragon-blood gives you, Dragandrea. My ancestors knew it, too."

He held out his hand.

"Give me the amber."

Alandis' hand covered the amber as it sputtered and sparked.

"This amber keeps my heart alive!" she said sharply. "I can't give it to you. It's only because it's assimilated into my bloodstream that it has any 'grace' with the dragons. Even if I could give it to you, it would do nothing but anger them for your possession of some of their ancestors' blood."

He withdrew his hand with a snort.

"So, you say, princess. You want to know the real reason the dragons have left Lharmeval alone of late? You didn't drive them off, *my lady*. There's a dragon that will change your view of them all. Then you'll part with the amber in a heartbeat."

That chill that had struck her before seemed to have solidified as much as the veining-amber, and it was much, much more than that of the iceberg.

She may well have done little of use.

The shipwrecks – all the ruins – and now the dragons' deaths—

She couldn't start killing the dragons –

Dragons never outweighed human lives, and if push came to shove, she would only protect one. Was U'Dell right?

Yet, whatever was capable of killing dragons was also a danger to man, and U'Dell implied that it was another dragon – a thought that made even the Vanaile's breath tremble.

The Vanaile was seething softly behind her, reading the amber's pulse.

"Vanaile . . . I speak by both the dragon's word and that of Scier and Maia. I *will* find out what's going on; then I will call to you, and together we will find the best way to end it. If it is human, I trust that you will not become like one of them, destroying those responsible?"

The Vanaile refused to answer but did not immediately dissipate into mist. The plinking of water and the rolling waves beneath their feet began to grow like a rumbling stampede of flood and beast.

Go, it breathed at last. *One chance, ice-heart, and if I feel that even one more is lost before you call to me, I will not be waiting.*

It melted into the ice.

Going with U'Dell was the last thing Alandis wanted to do. But Solavier *couldn't* be far behind!

Alandis turned to U'Dell.

"I . . . will go with you," she heard herself say reluctantly.

Solavier, where are you?

XI

A Knight for a Knight

Even the wind was silent in the north.

Alandis kept her eyes fixed on U'Dell as she kept him riding before her, the jingling of their horses' tack ringing statically between each hoofbeat on the damp earth. The snow was missing here. Nothing grew except the crumbling gray of lichen, spattered red as if by drying blood. Night was falling swiftly, leaving a dreadful red and gold glow in the west.

There was no whispering of voices in the snow, for there was nothing but a dim dust of white on the mounds of stone and lichen, but Alandis' fears kept whispering, fears of the ghosts of those on the shipwrecks. She didn't even know whether they had perished. She had to earn the Vanaile's trust and keep it from attacking again.

If U'Dell was right. . . she had to find a way to kill the dragons before they killed her people.

If the Vanaile was right. . . she still had to find a way to keep it from killing her people and to find those responsible.

She didn't know what U'Dell was taking her to see, save that he had implied it was a dragon. She didn't know where it was. Why would a dragon kill its kin? And if it wasn't a dragon – or if it wasn't a dragon that U'Dell was taking her to see –

She felt her fingers sliding back towards her seica. She didn't trust U'Dell within an inch of her life, yet here she was, following him into a territory she had next to no knowledge of, to face what, exactly, he hadn't said.

They would ascertain whether it was a dragon which was killing the others – that was her suspicion, not U'Dell's; he just wanted them all dead. Was he somehow responsible? But how would he kill a dragon? Did the Knights of Marén know more than this one was telling?

She clutched at the amber.

There was some use of the amber he wanted, and he seemed willing to cause her death to stop the dragons.

But then, hadn't she been willing, too?

If it was a dragon, what then? What could they possibly do to stop it? If there was something, perhaps U'Dell would direct her how to use the amber – but she wasn't sure she wanted to trust him then, either.

Something about the black knight made every nerve rattle her like a vampire's ghost.

Sol had not yet appeared, despite Alandis' glancing back every few moments to scan the horizon.

There was no chance that Solavier would be so far behind of his own will.

She narrowed her eyes at the scythe on U'Dell's back, barely sheathed by stiffened hide marked with a sickly weave of ochre and seaweed-green.

There were only four things she knew for certain:

The Vanaile had wrecked the ships and was of a mind to kill humans, if it hadn't started already.

U'Dell couldn't be trusted.

A dragon-war had to be avoided, and her people protected.

And *something* had happened to Solavier.

"How did you get away from Solavier?"

U'Dell didn't bother turning around to see her eyes fixed on him.

"How do you think I got this?"

He pulled the plating from his forearm, revealing a bloody gash that was growing black.

Alandis seized his sleeve.

"I asked you! What have you done to him?"

He shrugged her hand off, adjusting the plating.

"He got in my way."

"U'Dell!"

Alandis was hissing nearly in his face, and U'Dell took the time to consider the resemblance between her and the Vanaile.

"He may be following us, or he's lying in the infirmary at Lord Arvan's house; or, he's lying at the bottom of the sea."

He waved his hand carelessly in the direction they had come.

Alandis' heart seemed to shrink, and she jerked her head back towards the horizon behind them – wherever he was, Solavier was days away – dead, dying, wounded? She gripped the reins, twining her fingers in Sissi's neck until the girl couldn't feel her fingers and the horse snorted in discomfort.

"Keep your mind on the matter at hand!" U'Dell said impatiently. "This dragon will be responsible for far more than one life if you don't stop it."

"How...*could you?* You didn't have to hurt him!" Alandis' whisper rose as if coming in from miles away.

"The Knights of Marén learn to do what they have to, as your knight also seems to follow, in his own way. Someone had to stop the dragon, and it was clear that it wasn't going to be either of you," U'Dell said grimly, finally twisting around in the saddle to face her better. His steely eyes didn't shrink from her wild ones.

"If I was certain I killed him, I would state so, for the Knights of Marén are not ashamed of what they have to do. Now listen to me, my lady, for the sooner we deal with this freak of nature, the sooner I can get you back to your knight. I know you hate to put one life on pause, but it's better than hundreds, or worse."

His gentle tone startled her. She released Sissi's mane, scrutinizing the man's face, barely holding herself back from jerking on her mount's reins and turning her around.

U'Dell was right, if he could possibly be right about anything, and she hated that either side of admitting it felt like betrayal.

Yet he didn't need to hurt Solavier to deal with the dragon!

She bit her tongue until she tasted the metallic hint of blood.

Sissi kept on northwards.

XII

Knight's Shade

The land stretched away, black under the moonless near-night. U'Dell and Alandis had kept on all through the changing of dusk to midnight, restless, for time was of the essence, and the country was too wildly silent to be safe.

Dawn came, defined only as the thinnest crack of musty yellow that clung to the horizon, shivering with the refusal to climb the sky and wipe away the dusky shroud of nightshade. They were past the northern boundary where the sun never seemed to rise above the horizon, leaving that blue-violet and gold glow persistently rimming the dome of the sky, the shadows drenching all like wine.

It was as dark in the day as in Alandis' heart. Every step and breath were heartbeat prayers. Her eyes were fixed now on Sissi's mane, feeling the heavy weight of the amber on her heart. Every tear that fell on its face seemed to fragment off of it, as the light sizzled and died.

She couldn't lose Solavier.

He was right – or was he? – that she shouldn't have gone.

The scraps of brush shuddered as the riders passed. The air held a foul warmth, only enough to notice, for it did not touch the ice-clad stones that clattered unsettlingly under the horses' hooves.

Rocks and ice were everywhere, and the land was completely barren – even the thin light didn't sparkle on the ice here, and the stars had been swallowed up.

Alandis felt a prickling of dread that briefly closed her thoughts. She had heard of this land, but the description did not match this.

"What are the shadows?" she whispered, unaware she'd spoken.

Dlam snorted softly.

"You shall soon find out, Dragoi- I mean, Dragandrea."

No more was offered.

The timeline ran through Alandis' mind –

The danger of her heart in childhood; the assimilation calling to the dragons; running away from home, pitching herself into the role of Dragandrea with the weight of her guilt; her interior struggles leading the Vanaile's attacks – what else had her emotions led? Her efforts to hold off the dragons had caused their death – triggering the shipwrecks – and led to Solavier's – death?

The amber spluttered as Alandis prayed that Solavier would survive, that she could end what she had begun.

It replayed over and over, searching for the first fault, always stopping on her heart: the one thing no one could have changed, the implant that had seemed so innocently salvific.

Sissi halted under the tightening reins.

How had he known? How had the doctor known what the amber had done? He could not have drawn the dragons during his experiments – but Dlam knew even more than she did.

U'Dell looked back, his face, though obscured, almost certainly impatient.

"How did Dr. Guéreur know that the amber drew the dragons here? How do you know this 'other use' of the amber?"

U'Dell snorted, staring ahead at the murky horizon.

"The 'good doctor' has a tale which he has done well not to tell. I don't mind ruining his reputation right now with some of it, seeing as it impacts you."

He paused. "Your Doctor Guéreur hadn't known of any possible repercussions when he had tested the implant, or even when he performed the surgery for you. Our people are familiar with the usage and assimilation of dragon amber, which served our ancestors well. You may not realize that Lharmeval was our hunting ground, so to speak, before your people came and walled us out. We collected amber here which assisted in protection from the second dragon-era, which infested our land."

"I thought Lharmeval was the only ancient home of dragons," Alandis interrupted. "That there's no sign of a dragon-based history in our surrounding lands."

Dlam's silence spoke volumes.

As the seconds ticked past, he muttered, "Signs can be misread, Dragandrea."

"I should have asked you what you're doing here in the first place. We first assumed you were on a pleasure ride, as some of your people do, for you're never sent on missions in Lharmeval and you're rarely alone. As you know, more than one, or one on a mission, is read as an act of aggression –"

"Perhaps another misreading."

"Of you? You seem . . . accurate," she muttered. "but . . . I think you only came because of the dragons. You wanted to kill them for glory, I think."

"Maybe. But it should be clear now that we both need the dragons dead."

Alandis dropped her head, still wondering.

"During the gap years in which I'm sure you lost track of him," U'Dell continued, "Guéreur had been an imprisoned citizen of Marén. Another note you'll appreciate is that he studied with us in his younger years. I know that's very nearly forbidden in Lharmeval. At this time, he learned some of what our ancient people knew of amber usage. Most information was kept under lock and key. When it was discovered that Guéreur performed an amber surgery in this realm, he was called back to us for a 'presentation,' a pretense to be questioned about Lharmeval's remaining supply of amber. We knew, of course, what would happen. Amber is the only way to protect from dragons, as you've found out. But Guéreur discovered too much amber lore that would have been . . . dangerous for him to practice. He was imprisoned and commanded to perform similar surgeries for our people: for reasons."

He paused as if weighing the weight of his words against the already heavy air.

"Those that received the amber mysteriously vanished, Dragandrea. Rumor spoke of a creature of shadow and blood. This is the beast we've come to see."

As Alandis stared at him, the ice cracked the air on their right. Alandis became conscious of a shadow moving through the rocks. She jumped with Sissi.

U'Dell raised his hand, holding Alandis still as Sissi danced, desperate to wrench free of the tight hold.

"There's nothing to fear, yet."

U'Dell hailed the shadow. As it drew towards them, the amber-light glinted off of armor.

It was black.

Alandis realized with a sinking heart that there were six copies of the helm of Marén, more ghoulish than knightly.

"My comrades," Dlam said, noting Alandis' expression, far too well-lit by the blazing amber. "I've asked them to meet us here. . . 'for reasons.'"

That was little more comforting. She shrank back as the knights were motioned to wall her in.

She was trapped within that black barricade that was scarcely distinguishable from the darkness around them. She eyed the knight on her left, who sat low in the saddle as if in injury, his right arm as stiff as U'Dell's had been during the ride.

The latter dropped a reprimand that such posture was unfit for the soldiers of Marén, but it changed little.

They rode claustrophobically close, hemming her in with the sound of metal shifting against metal, U'Dell now two lengths ahead of her.

Alandis felt distinctly that this was not protection, but imprisonment. Her thoughts swirled, trying to find the truth in U'Dell's words, the implication that, perhaps, Doctor Guéreur was not the friend she had believed him to be.

Alandis tightened her lips. Regardless of Guéreur's past and the purpose of this escort, she would see this cryptid and make her judgment. She would halt it, if it were in her power. She would protect Lharmeval and return to heal Solavier.

So she said.

They came to a shallow pit that had been dug beneath a rimming formation of boulders, the remnants of a mountain which had once been crushed by some prehistoric meteor.

"There!" U'Dell announced, freezing them all. "Dragandrea, we'll leave our horses here. The rest of you will wait."

Alandis grimaced at him, studying the faint outline of the walled channel that dug beneath the rocky bank.

"My Lady! I've told you that I'll get you back to aid your Zain once this monster has been taken out. You know it needs to be done, and we need you."

The knight on Alandis' left hand half straightened, drawing a breath to object. U'Dell silenced him.

"Black Knights tend not to be so . . . consoling as I might be at times. I see you need it."

The war chargers pawed impatiently under their riders' hands as they delayed to move aside, drawing another sharp glance from U'Dell.

"Remember!" he snapped but gave no clue what exactly was to be remembered.

Slowly, they peeled apart.

"Dismount," U'Dell commanded, and walked ahead into the darkness.

Alandis dropped from Sissi's back. One of the knights took hold of the halter. Alandis strode silently ahead, feeling for the rocks on either side, probing for any that might be in her path.

If there was a time to regret the existence of gravel, it was now. Even the most careful steps were as good as a doorbell to a dragon's ears.

Alandis didn't find any rocks, but she did run into Dlam. The edge of his pauldron cut her cheek. The amber glowered.

"Watch it! Cover that thing, will you?"

Alandis settled her cloak higher over her shoulders, twisting it to fully dampen the light. U'Dell grasped her arm and pulled her over a straggling wall.

A gasp wrenched its way out of Alandis' throat. They stood now within the natural amphitheatre, the walls piling up behind them, blocking out the sky, but a lurid glow coated the ground underfoot: bloody orange, dimly flickering, illuminating the carcasses of not one dragon, but twentyfold. The spitfires, tzaidra, swamp wyrms, drakes of each species, and another Vanaile, their bodies collapsed as if the very breath had been sucked out of them, the color turned to ash in a puddle of folded skin and scales, each with a three-pronged piercing in a limb or the neck.

It was as if the dragon-blood had been drained into the earth, leaving the final vestige of energy to die in the soil.

"As I have said. . . you'll soon part with the amber in a heartbeat," U'Dell said grimly, tightening his hold on Alandis' arm.

There was a gaping maw at the opposite end of the amphitheatre, a den, Alandis suspected.

"If. . . you've seen this thing before, how did you escape?"

"It was busy with a dragon. Now it's nearly run out, out of all the ones that weren't smart enough to hide away. It cloaks itself in the shadows it creates. It may well be on top of us before we hear a sound or see a single scale –"

A bone fell from the ribs of a tzaidra, landing with a thunk and a final spark that skittered across the stones.

U'Dell stopped speaking, fixing his eyes on the tzaidra's hide, but Alandis felt the shivers in her spine drawing her gaze to the opposite side of the amphitheatre, where the shadows were impenetrable, as if all matter had vanished.

She pulled on U'Dell's arm, but at that point he didn't need to be told.

Whatever dim light the sky held was swallowed as a shape materialized, completely blackened, save for the dim glow as of a single angered ember.

The cryptid of Marén.

Smoke and shade curled out of it, a sliver of silver rimming its massive form like the tearing of an eclipse, as if it had sucked the moon and stars from the sky, like nothingness framed – in truth it was incomparable to any dragon, a vampire of its species, drinking of the dragon-blood that grew it beyond an imaginable measure –

Its eyes were the fuming, furious red of a fiery death, the last thing any of its victims saw, as the dragon's wings burst into flame.

The killer of dragons, soon to drain all of Lharmeval.

Any prayer didn't make it into known words as Alandis stumbled back, eyes darting in search of any sign of weakness – surely some scale had to have been loosened, the dragons would have fought!

U'Dell still held her arm, watching the dragon's jaws cracked open.

"Only your amber can put a chain on this one."

"It has no missing scale!"

He turned slowly to her.

The firelight turned his eyes to acid.

"But you do."

XIII

The Eye and Sickle

Where does your focus and horizon go when you're trapped between a traitor, a sinking heart that knew better, and an unholy terror?

Alandis didn't know, either.

Wide eyes willing to be confused, she jerked her head to the vampire that threatened, clawing its way closer, beginning to shrink the sky as green lights began to flash, the beauty of the aurora out of place, for once.

Why hadn't the other dragons sent out a distress signal, their location, if they were all interconnected?

Her heart skipped a troubled beat.

There had been no time.

Her head jerked backwards.

There was no time for her, either.

Her presence of mind snapped back. She could try speaking to it, futile as it might be.

Dragon! Hear me out, let me speak to you!

The amber's voice shook and shrank into the shadow and no answer came. Alandis shuddered, praying. She didn't want her family to find out about her role as Dragandrea, not by tale of her veins being drained as the fallen dragons' blood and bones had been!

"U'Dell! What do I have to do with the amber?"

"If it doesn't waste its time on us, it goes out to hunt the dragons it couldn't lure – and maybe your people, and the world after. Apocalypse. Choose wisely."

He was maddeningly passive and measured, eyes fixed on her, not on their predicament.

"That didn't answer my question!"

"Give it to me."

Alandis threw him a despairing look, increasingly aware of the tick-tocking seconds, that at the next moment they would probably be dead.

"*I can't.* Just tell me what to do! The amber needs to be alive –"

She froze. His eyes were still glowing with the smoke of the vampire, and the green bands of light that wove overhead.

"Does it. The dragon needs to die. Give me the amber."

"U'Dell! Stop wasting time! What on earth are you doing?!"

Dlam was watching the dragon, or the visible shred of it.

"You have. . . ten seconds."

"This is a trap, isn't it. You are what we thought you were!"

"Oh, I was right about the dragon, as you can see. But, I also want you dead. Unfortunately for you, your guilt makes you gullible."

He moved towards her, languidly tracing the edge of a sickle, blackened steel with an inset of jade and jet.

"You see, there is more at work here than saving your people, Adrastèja. We of Marén intended to turn the dragons into the greatest war machines that none but our ancestors have seen, and it can only be done via living amber. I needed you because amber is not available in Marén, only in Lharmeval! Our predecessors used the amber to enslave the first dragons, to wipe them out when they broke free, but the ancient relics have been drained from overuse. It was ill fortune, particularly for you, when the Doctor's techniques could not speed up assimilation quickly enough for all of our Black Knights. You see why I need your amber, and your dear *èskalak* out of the way. But I also want your title, so I don't mind if it kills you."

"U'Dell! Now is *not* the time for monologuing! It's going to kill both of us!"

"Oh, but it is; and it will be you first, 'human dragon,' unless you give me the amber. You'll still be saving your people, Dragandrea."

Alandis was backing away, shaking her head. How could she survive this time? What had possessed her – but she didn't need to ask. She grit her teeth and turned her eyes to the passage in the rock. She would take her chance – but U'Dell's smirk said that he wouldn't give it to her.

"No, I can't – U'Dell, just tell me what to do – Dlam, no!"

But he threw his shoulder into her, hurling her to the ground – her wrist snapped against a shard of scale as she tried to break her fall, and Dlam crushed her back into the stone, pressing the wind out of her lungs.

"How does it feel to be trapped in a cage with your wings clipped? If only you hadn't taken me seriously."

"Dlam – no – time! It'll – kill – both of us," she choked, trying to kick him away as he strove to force the seica out of her hands and reach the amber, still hidden by the dove clasp.

The dragon was looming over them, watching as a goading spectator.

"Actually, just you, my lady. He knows I've lured some of the dragons here for him. Now, he just wants you, before he finishes off the hunt."

Alandis, frustrated by his insanity, finally got a knee free and into his ribs, using the seica to twist him off her as she jumped back and ran for the passage. She heard a clamor, clearly that of the knights, as they came running down.

The vampire had other thoughts. Its wing lashed out, claws digging up and throwing down boulders that were the height of ten men. They clattered and crashed, drowned by the dragon's eerie silence. The sloping alley disappeared, every breath of air stifled in stone, leaving only the shattered arena that tipped back anyone who strove to mount it.

If the knights had any intention of helping, which was doubtful, despite hearing a metallic voice calling her name, they were blocked. The amphitheatre rim rose high and jaggedly steep, even on the other side, insurmountable without a roundabout hike.

What Alandis didn't see, as U'Dell's arm wrenched around her neck with daggered-sickle in hand, was a growing ice-blue glow in the south, ringed by fire.

"Are you *insane*?" Alandis gasped, trying for any method of freeing herself, desperately leveraging her seica, pushing the sickle away from her neck.

U'Dell struck a nerve on her right arm, pressing it deftly, and the seica dropped, clattering on the stones.

"Clearly."

"Well, thanks! Now that you've admitted that, quit choking me, because despite what you think you're not safe, and you don't have a way with dragons!"

"Actually, I do, with this one. You see, dear lady, it was when the other knights began disappearing that I discovered the Shade feeds on other dragons. I lured its prey here to earn the title of my ancestor – yes, the only true dragon-fighter, the *Dragjauna*, your legendary predecessor in title, came from Marén! I would do him and my people proud! I would have left only the best, the ones not weak enough to cooperate with you ... which means only the Shade and the Vanaile. You don't know how to control them."

The tip of the sickle pricked her throat.

"I told you this was a man's job, not a maiden's. At any rate, the Shade tolerates my presence, though I was forced to stop my baiting when I realized the Shade is the last of the primordial *vampyyri*, that it drains the precious amber into itself, save that which bleeds into the ground."

"If I'm to enslave it, I need you," U'Dell continued, voice low. "I need living amber that's already within human veins; even if you remove it, it will hold its power long enough for me to use it. I'm afraid you wouldn't have the strength to do so, but I do. Yes, I wrecked your confidence to guilt you into action. Yes, you're a gullible one, Dragandrea, a scarred one. . . about to be beyond repair. But you can still save your people, if you give me the amber. Your life for many, Dragandrea."

Alandis was staring past the blade as the shadows reassembled, and a chilling breath was on her face. The dragon was, in fact, waiting for U'Dell's cue. It didn't know what he wanted.

Scier, help me! Can this be what You want?

"Until Marén crushes them?"

"They may not be dead, Dragandrea."

A scream cut the air, a fire-winged roar that was braided by ice. For a single instant the entire landscape burned in daylight that was fire and ice crashing into opal, and the shadow shrieked in challenge only for a meteor to crash into the amphitheatre's heart. Ice cracked upwards, shattering into the neon sky as fire ripped across the ground.

The dust smashed upwards, filtering the blinding glow as the shockwave sent U'Dell and Alandis reeling backwards.

Betrayer of our race, how long did you think you could hide in your shadows and pin the blame elsewhere? Your blood-price will pay for the screams that have shattered my kin!

Alandis' jaw dropped, for that meteor was the Vanaile, and Mother, and Draco! The amber – it had been troubled by U'Dell long enough for them to trace her on the path to the darkened north!

Scales rattled upwards, baring moonlit veins, and fire and steam choked the air.

The vampyre turned its eye to them full on and threw its jaws open in a silent roar that shook the ground a second time.

The dragons were dwarfed, but not deterred.

Hardly had the Vanaile challenged the vampyre than all four beasts lunged for throat and tail, as the shade flitted in and out of physicality, infuriated, yet gloating at so many fish in a single catch . . . the remaining dragons that could not be lured had come.

All four.

Relief sent adrenaline out of Alandis in a bubbling flood, leaving her shaking, hoping that her dragon friends could hold their own against this monster –

Wait

She had forgotten U'Dell.

The dove clasp that shielded the amber cracked in two.

The sickle pared the amber implant as if it were frozen gelatin.

Her scream cut the air and hung there, alien, foreign to her, never drawn by fire or fear, drowned out by the thunder of dragons.

"ALANDIS!"

She didn't hear that call, didn't see the knights that had forced their way impossibly over the rim, didn't notice as one covered that ground at inhuman speed and ripped U'Dell off her before the sickle could pry out the amber's roots.

Half of the amber came out in U'Dell's hand as the pair tumbled, one up on his feet again at once, but Alandis didn't see him tear off the Marén helm, didn't see the blue eyes that blazed and the hair that burnt gold and bronze in the firelight, didn't feel the stone and scale that rushed up to meet her, crushing into her shoulders as she hit the ground.

Rivulets of fire
Amber, solid, molten, bleeding
Ice creeping, reverberating in every nerve
Her heart shuddered, screaming, crashing inward
Her vision blurred in flame

She didn't feel someone cradling her, the soft, broken words of the voice that had let her leave home, telling her to stay.

XIV

Dlam's Pyre

Crashing rolls of thunder rippled the sky overhead, lightning ripping through the shadows and blinding the aurora. The wind of the dragons' wings nearly swept the men off their feet as it howled through the amphitheatre.

Scale screeched against scale, tossing sparks, but the light lasted only a breath more as Trys' eyes blazed into U'Dell's.

The unknightly picked himself up.

Amber oozed like honeyed blood, dripping through his clenched fingers. The initial shock gave way to a smile curved and cruel like his sickle.

"You're really too late," U'Dell hissed softly.

Eyes ignited behind the wall of fire and steam and shadow. Draco swerved towards them, flames curling at every breath.

Trys didn't turn his head. His eyes only turned to the amber that had been ripped from Alandis' heart.

Solavier, limping, bandaged arm frustratingly in the way, shook off Zain Darje's support.

"Get to her," he rasped, and wished that he wasn't the one who might have a say against the dragons.

For her sake.

He blocked Draco's path to Trys.

"Eyes on me, Draco!" Sol snapped his blade against the raised paw. The drake shifted his weight, moving into a backwards prowl as he shifted focus onto Solavier.

U'Dell found his plan already going awry.

"What the heck, Vanaile!"

The same was still at the vampyre's throat. U'Dell snorted and squeezed the amber in his frustration. Thanks to his opponent, there wasn't enough of it to control more than one dragon-mind at a time. Draco was not the one for this job. He had too much feeling for Solavier to do much of anything.

"Well, that's a pain."

If he was going to do something about it, he didn't have a chance to make the shift.

Trys had no need of foresight, but his eyes caught every move ere U'Dell made it. Swifter than even the most skilled of warriors, with a strength equally surpassing, he was not the one U'Dell wanted to face. The broken rules of the black knight worked against Solavier, but not against the Ahren. Trys evaded every blow, landing his own well without a need to cut down, despite what his eyes said.

An outpouring of flame bathed them as Draco screamed at Solavier. It was a blessed thing that Marén armor was forged from the ancient history of dragon-fighting. Rather than risking transformation into an oven, it protected the wearer from the worst of the heat, and the embedded diamond slivers on the outer shell were a lifesaver when it came to tooth and claw.

Trys seized his chance as U'Dell shielded his face from the heat. Plunging forward, Trys hooked the sickle around the plating at U'Dell's neck, jerking him forward, dropping a sharp blow on his right wrist as he did so.

The amber dropped, unprotected, leaving only remnants coating U'Dell's glove.

Draco pulled up short and shook his head to clear it, giving U'Dell a scathing shriek of indignation.

"Draco! Shield Alandis, if you understand me," Solavier ordered, and the wincing wave he gave in

Alandis' direction might have helped clarify. The drake bounced off towards the fallen and her father and took up his place with worried gaze as his mother gave the vampyre a piece of her mind.

There was a thought that flitted through them all like a ghost, as legend crashed into reality, and vampyric habits became a truth –

As long as the vampyre had access to dragon-blood, ever since its awakening from century-slumber, it had no taste for anything else.

But if it drained Alandis – she would be dead, and it would have a new taste for human blood.

Trys threw the knight backwards, sending him crashing into the bones of one of the tzaidra.

Trys' heart ached, for the life of Alandis' heart was there, draining into the rubble. He stooped to catch it up.

U'Dell kicked out at Trys' jaw. Unsurprised, Trys blocked and flipped him as Solavier abandoned Draco to find the amber, but in that one breath, another knight ran into the space and blocked him in turn, kicking the amber back into U'Dell's hand.

"At least one of you is real!" U'Dell grimaced.

"If 'sir' Majagh hadn't gone galivanting off last week, we would have gone unchecked, and you'd

have six of us instead of a penta of bloodhounds!"
Orlan snapped, backing up to him as Solavier
turned on him, seething, and Zain Darje joined the
fight.

"I'll teach him to *use* his head instead of losing
it," U'Dell grumbled, narrowly ducking as scales of
rainbow hues, each as large as a shield, hurtled
through the air. "But let's see what I can do with the
Vanaile, shall we?"

Half the noise ceased as the Vanaile turned icy
eyes to the fight taking place below. Its seemingly
pupil-less eyes fastened on Trys and Sol, but only for
a moment.

What U'Dell wanted was amber. *All* of it. It
started for Alandis.

"Oh no, you don't!" Trys growled.

"When there's no bait, become the bait," Solavier
muttered, sizing up the Vanaile as it abandoned
Mother, and Draco went, shrieking, to her aid.
"Stick with these two, Trys, Darje! Oy, Vanaile!

The armor may have protected against fire; ice
and steam, however, it was not crafted to combat. It
may have been lucky that Solavier didn't know this,
or he might not have taken the risk.

He allowed himself to be snatched up in the Vanaile's claws, only to slam the pommel of his sword into the Vanaile's eye. Solavier crashed into the ground as the dragon dissolved beneath him. Steam scalded his face as he ripped off the helmet to free his vision.

Heaving breaths of steam began to roll like the ceasing storm, gushing over and cloaking everything in a heavy, sparkling mist. The ground was water, boiling, burning, breaking up, bubbling and churning, swirling the broken scales, threatening to throw the men off their feet.

"Stand still!" Solavier yelled at them. Even U'Dell froze. He might be in control. Or maybe he wasn't, for that steam and boiling ice would kill him in the same instant it killed Solavier, if he was the one who moved. Ice spikes slammed upwards, penning them in as it hunted for the Zain. Solavier took the risk and struck the water with his blade.

In that brief window Darje pounced on Orlan, knocking him flat into the lake. Trys snatched up one of the heavy scales and heaved it towards U'Dell. It struck him in the ribs, crushing his breath out of his lungs and denting his armor, leaving him on the ground. The amber dropped, and this time, there was no one to take it from the safety of Trys' hands.

Solavier jumped back as the Vanaile rose in front of him, drawing the lake within itself. It gave him a measured look as if biting its tongue before turning back.

Mother and Draco threw up their wings, blocking the jaws of the Shade, wings tearing beneath tooth and claw. The shadows kept vanishing, striking from the darkest corner.

"Sol, get this back to –" Trys dropped the amber into Solavier's hands but didn't have a chance to finish.

Clawing the air madly, teeth sank into scales as the vampyre flailed through the air, spattering the stones purple with its blood, keeping the vampyre from dematerializing.

It spread shadow like an ink cloud until the only visibility was the light of Alandis' amber, the dying breath of it from the edge of the crater, and the one in Sol's hand. He cupped his hands over it, seeking to cease the escaping rivulets, weapons forgotten.

Mother lost Draco in the cloud and called out for him, her voice ringing off the rocks, only to die in the shadows.

The men were stumbling. They could hear the shifting stones under the dragons' paws, but only when they were almost on top of the knights. No one could hear anything as more than a whisper.

That is, until Draco screamed. Fire exploded as the Shade sank its fangs into his shoulders to replace the spilling energy from its wound. The poison that was the shadow was full of air, a shadow of strength, leaning far, too far on the edge of freshly spilling amber.

Mother screamed in fury as she felt the attack on her son echoing in her own veins. The Vanaile hissed and with an arch of its back, shed thousands of diamond ice crystals into the cloud, catching on the hulking shape –

Mother released every ounce of fire within her.

The Vanaile's white eyes caught Sol's as it plunged into the darkness. The amber echoed in the Zain's hands as it caught its last words.

Tell her, èskalak, she isn't an ice-heart.

Of one mind the dragons pounced on the Shade in its vulnerable moment, its jaws still latched onto Draco's throat.

Lava collided with ocean spray in a roar that sucked the shadows away, creaking, cracking, and hardening. Screaming, the lava poured over the ground – a black claw reached for a hold but found U'Dell instead.

"*Orlan!*"

But his cry was drowned with the last flash of fire, drowned, not in shadow, but in stone, as Orlan watched in horror. The ice, too, was gone, leaving the air ringing in silence.

The curling steam faded away, and blackness crowded out the sky once more. A monolith of stone rose voicelessly. At its foot lay Draco, his breath weak, faded, but not drained.

The last of the dragons survived.

The men stood there, dazed, until Ean called to them angrily.

Turning, they found Ean and his father cradling Alandis. She was fading like the dragons whose carcasses lay torn and charred. Her fingers grasped weakly at the soil, unknowing and unfeeling as her father helplessly watched the amber pour out, her blood pouring with it.

"No, no, no!" Ean moaned. "Why did she leave?"

"Little, little Dove, you were supposed to come home! Don't leave us –"

Trys dropped beside them, gently turning Alandis' head from her father's shoulder, to see the raw red wound where the broken amber remained partially embedded, like a gaping maw struck through honeycomb.

"Mielė! You mustn't leave us again!"

Adrastėja raised pleading eyes to Trys.

"Help her," he whispered. "You have some grace as an Ahren. Please give it to my little girl!"

Trys didn't answer. His eyes belied his uncertainty. None of them had ever known exactly what "broken" meant, when it came to Alandis' implant. All they knew was that it would be the kind that couldn't be repaired, the gaping wound that only love and safety could soothe.

Alandis' eyes were half-open, barely conscious, but unseeing. The color had left her face, blue veins networking like streams against snow. Her heart scarcely beat.

"Sol, the amber!"

Taking it from the hand outstretched, he pressed the shard into the implant's brace, where it scarcely seemed to fit now. He cupped his hands over the stone, breathing softly in the Ahren tongue a prayer of grace and sunlight, that the grace of the sunlight infused in him might fuse the stone and save the heart that had relied on the sun. He smoothed the runny amber over its surface, filling the fractures. Slowly, the trickling stopped.

The amber was one piece. One, but cracks meandered as on winter ice. The glow was dimmer than it had ever been. All the assimilated amber had broken from her veins, mingling with that already spattered over the amphitheatre's surface. The amber in her hair had bleached to peach and rose.

She didn't stir. Trys paled. He turned his eyes to Adrastėja, for once becoming the one who seemed lost in a storm.

Solavier was breaking at the sight of Alandis, memories of the Vanaile and fluttering doves driving it in.

"I shouldn't have let her go! Why did I let you go?"

His voice cracked, barely audible in the widening stillness.

Lana – I made you make a promise you couldn't keep!

Her father said nothing; Ean said nothing either, but his eyes fell on Solavier with a pained look that echoed.

"None of us should have," Trys whispered. "She ran because she thought she hurt me, and I was only fearing to hurt her."

The aurora had stopped overhead. Stars crept out of the veil at last. The ice of the Vanaile lingered on the cold air, weighted as the words.

"I hate to be the one to say it," Zain Darje said quietly. There was no need for him to pin down the silent Orlan, who stood, watching dumbly. "You needed to. She needed to come, to make that . . . stop."

No one needed to turn to see the monolith he referred to; no one did.

No one needed to elaborate or to connect.

The faintest movement against Trys' hand opened his eyes.

"Alandis?"

The color was still lost. The hand that longed to move and find if his face was really there, if he were really there, could not. Her hazy eyes strove to focus on his face, fighting dimly against sleep as her lips trembled against the wave of pain.

"Trys?"

"You didn't have to run from me, Mielė," he breathed, and a tear dropped on her cheek. "I thought you knew that I'm always going to come when you need me, little Dove! I should have known your fears . . ."

"Trys? The dragons –" Crying, she tried to move her head as she remembered, and remembered the shadow that had been looming over her in her last moments awake.

Her father smoothed her hair.

"Everything is alright now, Dove! Everything."

"They – told me – I'd be broken," she trembled, tears spilling.

"Then it's good that there are people who love you enough to hold you together," Trys whispered, and lifted her into Solavier's arms.

A gasp cut through her tears and Sol bent over her, holding her close as the tears were muffled into his shoulder.

"Sol, Sol, he – I thought he killed you – I'm sorry!"

"Just don't leave!"

About the Author

Thérèse Judeana is a young traditional Catholic with a love for fantasy, believing, like Tolkien and C.S. Lewis, that sometimes it holds a secret key to drawing the soul towards the true reality of God. An accomplished writer, she creates both science-fantasy worlds and fairytale lands. Thérèse lives in Central Florida, where she attends the traditional Latin Mass with her family. Currently, she is studying fashion design and fashion history, designing her own wardrobe, and working on her publications, *Windflower* and *Aesthété*.